J. B. Rideout

Six Years on the Border

J. B. Rideout

Six Years on the Border

ISBN/EAN: 9783337344627

Printed in Europe, USA, Canada, Australia, Japan

Cover: Foto ©Andreas Hilbeck / pixelio.de

More available books at **www.hansebooks.com**

Six Years on the Border;

OR,

SKETCHES OF FRONTIER LIFE.

BY

MRS. J. B. RIDEOUT.

———————

PHILADELPHIA :

PRESBYTERIAN BOARD OF PUBLICATION,

1334 CHESTNUT STREET.

WESTCOTT & THOMSON,
Stereotypers and Electrotypers, Philada.

CONTENTS.

SIX YEARS ON THE BORDER.

CHAPTER I.

FIRST EXPERIENCES.

MY object in this narrative is to give my Eastern friends an idea of life on the Western plains—not such an idea as the tourist forms while riding over these great prairies in the swift-moving cars and stopping a few days in the different towns and villages, but such a one as is gained by those who live on the extreme border, and thus prepare the way not only for railroads and cities, but for civilization and good society. History tells us of the trials of our forefathers—their battling with sickness, cold and hunger, their deadly conflicts with the treacherous Indians—together with their firm, unshaken faith in the God whom they worshiped; but how many of their posterity whose names and labors of love are never written for the benefit of those who come after them have passed through sorrows and dangers as great as theirs!

In my quiet New England home, during my youthful days, I never dreamed of being a minister's wife or of passing through scenes which to many of my readers may seem incredible. But the young cannot see the path which God has marked out for them to walk in through this wilderness of life. After we have gone forward for a number of years, and then look back, how many exclaim, "He has led me in a way which I knew not"!

In the month of August, 1871, I left my Eastern home, friends and many surroundings that were dear, especially the graves of loved ones, which I never expected to see again, and started for the Far West—a journey of twenty-five hundred miles. But it was not without scattering tears over places which memory held so dear, that I bade farewell to friends; and after weeping over the graves of my mother and darling babe, I turned my back upon the scenes of my childhood, and with my husband and two small children began my long and wearisome journey.

After traveling day and night for ten days, I found myself beyond the clatter of engines and the sound of " the church-going bell." But "Onward! Onward!" was our motto. We had heard of a village on the banks of a beautiful river, surrounded by a rich country fast filling up with intelligent people, but with no one to proclaim the glad tidings of salvation, and to that town we were going with bright hopes of happiness and usefulness. But long before we reached our destination my heart grew faint and my own native New England seemed dearer than ever before. Our conveyance was a little open wagon drawn by two small ponies which were very unruly; and the driver, on account of a bottle which projected from the pocket of his old brown jacket, was no better than the ponies.

There were many deep ravines and streams without bridges to cross, and several times I sprang from the wagon, with my little girl of two years in my arms, to see our trunks go tumbling down into some ditch. The driver seemed to be perfectly unconcerned over our misfortunes, and occasionally would say, " You'll soon get used to this if you stay in the West." This was early in the month of September, and the dry grass in many places was much higher than the horses' heads, and as far as I could see in every direction this dry brown coat of nature was waving in the wind, which blew furiously, and to me seemed almost unearthly on account of its parching heat. Occasionally we would pass a little cabin, but no barns, no fences, no orchards, no springs; and, what gave the country a more desolate appearance, there were no trees except a few dwarfed cottonwoods, which scarcely lifted their topmost branches above the ravines in which they stood.

Being very thirsty, I called at one cabin, and as I looked in I started back with horror. There were three or four invalids lying on blankets which were spread on the ground; for the cabin had no floor and was so open that a cat could enter between the logs. The woman of the house said, "We are all sick here." I asked for a drink of water, and she pointed to a ravine in which stood a stagnant pool, and said, "There is the water we use." I turned away thinking I could never drink such water as that. But as I saw the driver dipping it up in his old hat and drinking it, I recalled what he had said before: "You'll soon get used to this if you stay in the West."

At last we reached the town of which we had read such glowing accounts before

leaving the East. My hands were brown,
my face blistered and my eyes red, and as
I stood in the village which had appeared
to my imagination in so many different
forms (but always with beautiful houses,
sidewalks and level streets), feeling home-
sick and discouraged, I looked around and
counted the buildings. One blacksmith's
shop, one small store, one dwelling-house
and two little cabins, and all surrounded
by the same brown, rustling mantle which
covered the whole region. As I looked
for the beautiful river, I saw a bed of sand
half a mile away, with a little stream, shal-
low and muddy as it is at that season of
the year, finding its way through the sand.
There was no hotel, but in one of the cabins we found a shelter; it contained but
one room, and had no floor. Besides the
family, consisting of man and wife and a
daughter nearly grown, there were three
gentlemen-boarders, and all down sick.

The first night we slept in that cabin I

thought of the one represented by Richardson in his "Beyond the Mississippi," where a man stands in the door saying to a stranger who desires admittance, "We are about full here." I soon began to learn what border life meant.

My husband began to preach the gospel and visit the sick. It being the malarial season of the year, there was scarcely a well person to be found in all the region. Whole families were suffering at once; so that one could not wait on the others. I went three miles from home with my husband to attend the funeral of a child. The mother was a refined, educated woman from Boston, and she said she had not been out of bed for six weeks, during which time all of her children had been sick and two of them had died, and not a woman had before been to see her. Her husband had been suffering with the chills until he was scarcely able to wait on his sick family. It is sad to see a whole family sick even when surrounded by kind friends to care for and comfort them ; but when father and mother and children are all sick in a strange land, and surrounded by invalids, God alone can sustain them.

In the midst of these scenes of poverty and suffering, where such an opportunity for usefulness opened before him, and where one possessed of health and strength felt such animation and delight in trying to relieve sufferers, my husband was taken suddenly and violently ill with a fever. What to do I did not know. A physician could not be had. One had just died with a congestive chill, and the other was very ill. I did the best I could. For nearly two weeks my husband had a burning fever day and night, during which time I endeavored to trust in the Lord ; and after caring for my husband, I did what I could for others. After he began to recover health he gained very rapidly. In four weeks from the time that he was taken ill he was able to walk around, and in a short time he began to visit the sick and preach the gospel "from house to house."

The nights were now cold and frosty, and people who survived the scourge were in most cases convalescent. In a short time we moved into a cabin by ourselves, and my husband commenced driving a team for wages, preaching every Sabbath in the different cabins. We were now comparatively comfortable, and were quite happy until the next spring.

Early in the month of April my husband was helping a neighbor plant corn, when, he said, all at once the hoe became so heavy he could scarcely lift it; his head pained, his arms were tired and his back ached. He finally concluded that he must be sick, but he continued to work until his teeth began to chatter, and he knew he was having a chill. He then came home, and after shaking for an hour or more he had a burning fever, and was quite sick

during the day. After this he had a chill
nearly every other day for six weeks, until
he was reduced in flesh almost to a skele-
ton, and was not able to do any labor. By
this time our money was all gone, and
about the first of June we had eaten our
last morsel of bread for breakfast. We
did not know where our dinner—if we
were to have any—was to come from. My
husband took a small sack and went from
house to house among those to whom he
had been preaching during the winter,
asking for the loan of a little cornmeal
(cornmeal and buffalo-meat were our prin-
cipal articles of food), but late in the afternoon he returned with his sack as empty
as when he had left home in the morning.
He was so faint, weary and hungry that he
lay down to rest. Our little children, who
had been waiting patiently for his return,
looked at the empty sack with much disap-
pointment, and without saying a word
walked away.

While he was resting many thoughts passed through my mind. I thought of leaving such a place of poverty and wretchedness, but we had no money. I thought of writing to some friend, but we would all die before I could get an answer. I then thought of the precious promise of Jesus: "Ask, and ye shall receive;" and I knew my husband was at the same time looking to our heavenly Father. Shortly after he arose from the bed, stepped from the cabin and walked over to the store. The man who kept it was away, but my husband told his wife that he was out of bread, and she pointed to a pile of flour and said, "Help yourself." I was surprised when I saw him return with a sack of flour, for I knew that the rule at the store was "Strictly no credit." We thanked God for his mercy in that our prayers were answered and we not forsaken.

From this time my husband began to improve, but continued to have an occasional chill, which kept him weak during the whole summer.

About the last of the month he heard of a town springing up in a very beautiful part of the country, forty miles farther west, and he resolved to go, if possible, to that place. He heard that there were some capitalists at the new town, and he thought that if he were once there he could get work to do and thus maintain his family. So he started away from home with only six cents, which was all the money we had. Our flour was nearly gone. I divided what was left, wrapping a loaf of bread in a paper for him to take and keeping a little for my children and myself. When he returned, he gave me the following account of his journey, trials and success:

"After traveling all day, riding part of the distance on a load of lime and walking the remainder, I stopped for the night in a little unoccupied house. I had divided my food with a hungry man during the day, and my bread was all gone. I had no blankets, but slept on the floor, using my boots for a pillow. Morning came and the sun was shining brightly, but I was in a strange land without anything to eat and with only six cents in money. I started on my journey; but, feeling faint, weary and almost discouraged, I went back to the place where I had slept, and after I had closed the door I went to one corner of the room and fell on my knees, determined not to arise until the load of sorrow and care should be removed from my poor depressed soul. I resolved to cast my burden on the Lord, for I knew that he was willing to bless and sustain me. I have often preached from the text 'There is a Friend that sticketh closer than a brother,' and I endeavored to claim that promise and look to that Friend for help.

"After I had unbosomed my sorrows to Jesus, and told him I was sick and hungry and a poor wanderer in a strange land and

2

had not money enough to pay for my breakfast, my soul was filled with peace. I felt
him to be very near, and I knew he would
help me. I started again, and had gone
only a short distance when I saw a man
coming from another direction. He hailed
me and asked me if I knew the way to the
new town. I told him that I did, and was on
my way to that place. The stranger said
he had a team, and if he could sell his load
of meal at the store a little farther on he
would give me a passage. I felt certain in
my mind that he would sell the meal; and
he did. I told him I was sick and preferred
to lie down in the wagon, and as I closed
my eyes to thank God for answering my
prayer I heard the crack of a whip, and we
were off for the town of H——. I would
have purchased a loaf of bread, but I had
learned that there was a toll-bridge on the
way, a little beyond the place where I spent
the night, and I expected to have to pay
five cents to cross the bridge; but, as the

man with whom I was riding paid the toll for his team, I was allowed to go over with him free.

"After going a short distance his boy looked around and asked me if I did not want a lunch. He said he had some corn-bread and molasses, and, bringing it forth, told me to help myself. It was now near the middle of the day, and I enjoyed that corn-bread and molasses as much as though I had been partaking of the bounties of a king's table. 'This poor man cried, and the Lord heard him and saved him out of all his troubles.'"

CHAPTER II.

LOOKING FOR A HOME.

"THAT night," continued my husband, "we camped out on the wild plains, and the following day, about 11 A. M., we were at the new town. But how disappointed was I again! There were two stores, a blacksmith's shop, and a short distance away a little house. I asked every man I could find if he wanted to hire a man to do any kind of work, but they all said 'No;' and, judging from their looks, they had no money to pay for work, or for anything but bread and quinine. After a while I found one man who said he had a well to finish; it was then twenty feet deep and some water in the bottom. I told him I would work in the well for

fifty cents a day; but after looking me in
the face I think he concluded I was not
able to do such labor, and said he thought
he would not employ me. I was much disappointed and wished myself back in N——
with my family, and concluded to get back
if I could. I accordingly found a man who
was going with a team to within four miles
of N——, and I asked him for a passage;
but he refused to take me, as I had not
money to pay him.

"I then walked away from the little town
—perhaps a quarter of a mile—and in the
tall, waving grass I knelt down and asked
my heavenly Father to take care of his
poor wandering child. After spending a
few moments in prayer, my mind was composed, for I knew my Father would still
care for me. I then returned peacefully
to the town, and went to the little house
before mentioned and asked for five cents'
worth of bread; and the woman of the
house gave me such a loaf for five cents

as I had never before known to be sold for twice that amount of money. I took that, and gave it to the man and boy who had given me my conveyance. I then told them if they would let me have some cornmeal from their wagon I would get some bread baked (they were not very good cooks), and they said they would be very glad if I would do so. I then took some meal and went back to the house where I got the bread, and told the lady if she would bake me some bread I would chop wood to pay her, as I had no money. She said she would be glad to do so, as her husband was sick.

"I had worked only a few minutes when a little girl came to the door and said her papa wanted me to come in. I walked in, and the man—an elderly man—said, 'You are sick, and not fit to be working out there in the hot sun. Sit down and rest until dinner is ready.' If any one had been near, they might have heard me say

'God bless you, old man!' I sat down in a rocking-chair for the first time in the West, and in a few moments I felt well acquainted with the strangers, who gave me much valuable information about the country and seemed to be very kind indeed.

"In a short time dinner was ready, and for the first time after leaving N—— I sat down at a table and partook of a good, wholesome meal. My friend then said I could take his horse and look around over the country. I thanked him, and soon, seated in a neat saddle, was moving over the prairie. After passing several cabins I saw one made of logs from which the bark had been peeled. It looked neat and clean. Seeing a man working at the door, I rode up and asked him if there were any vacant claims near his place. Without answering my question, he asked, 'Have you a family?' I told him I had a wife and two children. He then asked me if I did not want to buy a claim. I told him I did not, because I had no money except one cent. He laughed, and asked me where I was from. I told him from Maine. 'Is that so?' said he. 'I am from Vermont.' I told him I thought he was a Yankee when he first spoke. He then said, 'There was a gentleman came out here last March, took a claim, hired a man to break five acres and plant it in corn—and the claim is a good one, with ten acres of timber; and a stream of water runs through it, so there will always be plenty of water—and then he went back for his family, and a few of us neighbors have been holding his claim for him. The other day we received a letter from him saying his wife was sick and he had given up coming West to live, and we could let some man with a family have his claim. Now,' he continued, 'I will show you the claim, and I would advise you to go right on and take possession of it at once.' He then saddled his horse, and

together we rode down the stream more
than a mile, and came to a beautiful piece
of corn—the best sod-corn I had seen.
He showed me the corners of the quarter-
section, and told me there were good
neighbors on every side, and asked me
how I liked it. I replied that it was excellent. He then said he would help me
build a cabin and let me have his team to
go after my family. I thanked him, and
told him I would be at his place next morning; and then we went back to the town.
To my joy, I met a young man just from
N——, with whom I was acquainted. He
said I must stop with him that night, as he
had a camping-outfit along with him. I
told him of my good fortune and that I
wanted to write to my wife, but I only had
one cent. He very kindly assisted me in
purchasing a postage-stamp. I then went
into the store and asked the clerk if I could
write a letter. He said, 'Yes, certainly,'
and gave me a sheet of paper and en-

velope. But I could scarcely write for joy,
I felt so much better than I did in the
morning, when the stranger refused to
give me a passage back to N——.

"That night I listened to the conversation of several old frontiersmen who were
sitting around the store, for the night was
beautiful and the air was fragrant with the
scent of a thousand varieties of wild flowers. I listened to those men's talk about
the deer and the buffalo and the wolves,
then numerous in that region. They also
talked about the country—said it was the
richest land in the world, and they thought
the country was settling up with an excellent class of people, and they would soon
have schools and churches. I concluded
that the people were far superior to those
at N——, and after thanking God for his
mercy and divine guidance I went to sleep,
and slept sweetly until morning.

"In the morning, after a breakfast of
bread, bacon and coffee, and a pleasant

little chat with my friend from N——, I
started for the cabin of the good Yankee
who had been so kind to me the day before. I found him all ready, with his horses
harnessed to his wagon ; and we were soon
in the timber cutting and drawing out logs
for my cabin. We cut logs about six inches
in diameter and twelve feet long, and peeled
off the bark. As he was a good axeman
and strong and well, we soon succeeded in
putting up the walls of a house. During
this time I was kindly entertained by my
friend and his family. Every night we
read the Bible and prayed together, the
doing of which seemed to unite us more
firmly in the bonds of Christian love."

While my husband was thus learning the
rough ways of the border I was living in
awful suspense. I had plenty for myself
and my children to eat. After he had gone
away the merchant's wife was very kind,
and seemed almost like a mother to me.
But I knew the dangers were many away

out on the plains, and that in the region he was exploring no man's life was safe. The red men were on the alert for scalps; the border desperadoes lived by murder and theft; there were bears and wolves and the deadly miasma; and the scarcity of bread and water seemed dreadful to me. I could only wait and pray.

After a week of this melancholy endurance my aching heart was lightened on receipt of the following letter:

"My DEAR WIFE: I have had a hard time since I left. I have suffered for bread, and yesterday, while riding over the plains, what would I have given for one moment at our old spring in Maine! I kept the six cents you gave me until I reached here this morning, when I paid out five for bread, and have just borrowed two cents to enable me to purchase a postage-stamp. Do not be discouraged: I am not. I believe we shall come out all right yet. I had a slight chill the day I left, but am feeling quite comfortable now, though not very strong. I have some prospects before me which are good, but we have been disappointed so many times I dare not say much about it to you just yet. Do not look for me until I come. Take good care of the children, and trust in Him who feeds the ravens and notices the fall of a sparrow."

After reading this letter, like Paul before entering Rome "I thanked God and took courage."

Three days after this, on the 4th of July, my husband returned looking better than when he left. The kind man who had assisted him in building his cabin offered to lend him his team, but my husband, knowing the route to be infested with Indians, and being unarmed, concluded that he would rather come on horseback. The horse he rode was blind and could not go very fast. On the way he saw a party of Indians coming toward him; he knew he could not keep out of their reach, so he looked to God and said, "Thy grace has brought me safe thus far : thy grace will bring me home." The Indians came very near, and one raised his gun and pointed it toward him ; but in a moment they turned their ponies and rode off in another direction.

After this we soon made arrangements to move to our new home. A neighbor who had a good team and was well armed was engaged to take us through, and we were to pay him in wood and in other articles which we could not move. The night before we were to start my husband came in and said, "I do not know what we shall do to-morrow ; the river is up, and we shall have to cross with our load in the ferry-boat." (This was a different and nearer route than the one he had traveled when going before.) "I have no money to pay the ferriage ; and then we must have something to eat on the way, and I

would like to have a pound of nails and
a board, to make a door for our cabin.
If I had five dollars, I could get along
nicely." Just then he said it came to his
mind that when in Maine he gave a poor
minister whose son was very sick five dollars, and the Lord had said he that gives
to the poor lends to him; and he prayed:
"Lord, help us." At that moment the merchant over the way, who was considered by
many to be the most selfish man in the
place, came in, and after talking a few
moments and wishing us good luck he
opened his pocket-book and handed my
husband something. It was quite dark
in the cabin, and my husband said, "What
is this?" and the old man said, "That is
something to help you along to-morrow;"
and stepped out, saying, "Good-night."
To our great joy, we found that the five
dollars had come; and we knew it was
God who sent it.

CHAPTER III.

THE CABIN ON THE PRAIRIE.

THE next morning we were early on the way to our new home. We started early, because we did not want to camp out on the wild plains between the two settlements. The day was very hot, and, although I was seated on the top of the load, the aroma of flowers, the bounding deer and the skulking cayote, the wild sunflowers bowing before the breeze, with beautiful birds singing in their branches, one after another claimed my attention; and, as no Indians appeared in sight, the day passed away quite pleasantly. The sun went down long before we reached the settlement, and with much dread we stopped in the open country for the night, but on account of weariness caused by the long day's ride we lay down on the ground and slept soundly until morning.

The next day, about ten o'clock, we reached the cabin of our good friends. Here I was received so kindly that I felt at home at once. The good woman of the house said I should not move into our cabin until the roof was on. As soon as I met her I knew by the expression of her countenance and the warm grasp of her hand that I had met a friend; and if ever any poor wanderer in the desert of this world felt the need of a friend, I did at that time. Nor was I disappointed, for soon we loved each other dearly. She called me her sister, and wrote to her friends in the East that she had found a sister. She was truly a refined Christian lady,

> "A perfect woman, nobly planned
> To warn, to comfort and command;
> And yet a spirit, still and bright,
> With something of an angel light."

3

Here I was kindly entertained for a week, when I moved to my little home. Mrs. G——, who seemed like a sister indeed, went with me, taking several things for my comfort.

To one coming directly from a wealthy country, the idea of living in such a place as our cabin would have been rejected with horror. It was a little over ten feet square inside, six feet high in the middle and four on each side, the roof covered with poles and grass and dirt, and in the middle a post resting on a flat stone supporting the roof. But it seemed good to me because I needed a home, and I could say, " This is our own," like the man that lived near us in a " dug-out," who said to his boys as he looked at the walls of pure earth, " *Boys, this is ours ;*" and my good sister, who, after camping out for several days and then moving into her little cabin as night came on and the wind began to blow and the rain came down in torrents, said, "Oh, isn't this nice ?"

After we had lived in our new shelter a few days, there came a heavy thunderstorm in the night, and in the morning the water stood about six inches deep in our cabin. The prairie all around was flooded. Our bedding was wet and muddy, and the dirt floor remained damp for several days, making the cabin very unpleasant.

My husband had by this time so far recovered his health as to be able to work all the week and preach twice on the Sabbath. He commenced his labors in the grove, and the people, who were thirsting for the water of life, came for miles to hear the gospel. Occasionally an old frontiersman would say, "This seems like former times." One man, after listening attentively, said that was the first sermon he had heard for ten years. Little half-clad boys would sit under the trees, apparently drinking in every word, and many of the young people gave their hearts to the Saviour.

But soon the malarial season commenced,

and my husband, my children and myself
would all have a chill the same day. One
day we all lay with a burning fever from
morning until night, not one of us able
to wait on the other. The sun shone with
scorching heat, and during the day we had
no water that was fit to drink. We should
not have suffered in this way had Mr. G——
and his wife been at home, but that day
they were absent with their team. Every
day when they were at home they came
bringing us fresh water from their well,
and very often a basket of light bread and
butter and cake, and sometimes a little
fruit, which they had brought from their
home in the East. One day, early in the
month of September, they did not come
as usual; we knew they were home, because we could see their wagon in the
yard. The next day, fearing that something was wrong, my husband went to
their cabin, and found them both sick ; Mr.
G—— had a burning fever and was in ex-

treme pain, and my good sister was lying in the bed unable to help herself in the least. My husband hastened back for me and then sprang on one of their horses and started for a physician. When the physician arrived, he said Mr. G—— had a very serious attack of bilious fever and his wife had paralysis. After this, for three weeks, we both stayed with our friends and cared for them day and night. In a few days the physician told my husband it was very doubtful if either of them would recover, but in three weeks Mr. G—— was much better and able to wait on his wife a little, and we returned home with the understanding that my husband would visit them every night and morning. But Mr. G—— continued to gain in strength, and in a few weeks was well. Mrs. G——, however, was not able to get out of her bed until the next spring.

During the three weeks that we took care of them it seemed strange that my husband, my children and myself were all comparatively well; neither of us had a chill during this time, while most of the people in the vicinity had suffered very much, and several had died.

After we moved into our cabin we were frequently visited by large snakes. My husband killed one almost seven feet long. They often came into the cabin, and even dropped down from the roof to our table. One night I felt something crawl over my bare foot; the next morning I killed it. It was a rattlesnake with four rattles. One of our neighbors slept on the prairie, and in the morning he found a very large rattlesnake coiled close to his side. People were quite often bitten by these reptiles, but seldom died from the effects, as most persons kept an antidote always at hand. I became so accustomed to the peculiar buzz of the rattlesnakes that it did not alarm me very much. I have often killed them, and have laughed to see ladies just from the East run and scream when meeting a snake of the most harmless kind. A lady who lived near us saw her baby, about nine months old, playing with a bottle; on picking it up she saw a little rattlesnake coiled in it. Upon inquiring how it came there, the older boys said they drove it into the bottle and corked it up, for they knew it would amuse Frankie; and they then told their mother they had several "lariatted" out in the field. We had a dog that hunted snakes and killed them wherever he could find them; but in a little while the poor creature became very stupid and badly swollen around the head and neck, and after several days of suffering he died.

When I had returned home from taking care of my friend, I often felt very gloomy and as nearly discouraged as woman ever became. My neighbors were nearly all sick, and my husband was working for food and clothing during the week and away preaching every Sabbath. But I endeavored to overcome my despondency by working very hard when I was able to work; and when I was not able, I would read my Bible and put my trust in my heavenly Father.

One day about the last of October I was sitting in our little cabin with my children when I heard some one speak outside. I opened the door, and to my horror I saw five Indians sitting on their ponies in a nude state, their bodies painted in various colors. In their hands they had rifles, and to their saddles were hanging bows, arrows and knives. The sides of their heads were shaved, and on the tops the hair stood erect. They looked at me, muttering something. I fastened the door and prayed to God to take care of me. After holding a consultation for some time they filled their blankets with our corn, then rode off toward the unsettled plains; and I can assure my readers I was not sorry to see them go. The next day I saw a very large party— more than a hundred—of them coming

right from the Indian Territory, which was
only half a mile away. I fastened the door
securely, took my twin-babies in my arms
to keep them quiet, and, with the other
children nestling close to my side, waited
in anxiety and dread; for I did not know
what they would do. They surrounded
the cabin, pounded on the door and tried
to push it open. They remained a long
while, talked very loudly and seemed to
be disputing with one another. Finally
they rode away. I was covered with perspiration, my heart beat very fast, and it
was a long time before I dared open the
door; but when I looked out, they were
not to be seen.

A family consisting of husband, wife and
seven children lived out in the open air
near us all summer with nothing but a
wagon-cover for a shelter. In the autumn
my husband helped the man build such a
cabin as ours, in which they lived during
the winter. At meal-time each took his

piece of corn-bread and buffalo-meat as he could get it; sometimes they had bread and no meat, and sometimes meat and no bread. At night the three oldest boys would lie down by the side of a hay-stack, and the father would take the fork and cover them with hay. The remainder of the family spread their bedding on the dirt floor, and thus had a shelter. This man and his wife were intelligent and educated people from the State of New York. The next summer they raised a good crop of wheat, and were soon doing well.

During the winter it was extremely cold; for over a month the wind blew almost incessantly from the north, and several inches of snow lay on the ground. There were some weeks in which but few dared to venture away from their own premises. Several froze to death; one poor fellow was found stiff in his bed. Some who were out hunting never returned, and numbers were so badly frozen that they died nearly as soon as they came back. While returning, one party of seven was overtaken by a dreadful storm. One lay down and said he could go no farther, when a young fellow took his revolver and told him that if he had given up he would put an end to his suffering at once. The man concluded to make another effort; and when they arrived at the settlement, the man who had rallied his comrade was so badly frozen that he went on crutches for six months, while the others received but slight injuries.

CHAPTER IV.

PREACHING IN A DUG-OUT.

ONE of my husband's preaching-places was a "dug-out." On the Lord's day when the cold winds would be sweeping over the prairie, waving the dry grass and swaying the leafless branches of the cottonwood and the elm, and when the ringing tongues of ten thousand bells were speaking with clear, musical voices from the high steeples of costly churches, calling large congregations to assemble within clean and decorated walls, where the sun smiled sweetly through windows of stained glass, to sit on cushioned seats with costly carpets beneath their feet, to listen to God's word,—a goodly number of rough, hardworking frontiersmen, with their wives and children, would gather in this damp, dark abode of poverty to listen to the same gospel and worship the same God, in the name of the same Jesus, looking for the same reward beyond the grave and beyond the stars. If God heard the prayers of his ancient followers when in the dens and caves of the earth, and in the catacombs beneath ancient Rome, he certainly can be sought and found in a "dugout" away on the Western border. But, ye who worship in costly churches, think of such a sanctuary as this : no windows, and sometimes so dark that the minister can scarcely see his congregation, the floor of earth and the walls and roof the same, and, instead of cushioned seats, round poles. But in just such churches as this are blessed thousands of souls who will doubtless sing praises to Him who brought them "out of great tribulation, having washed their robes and made them white in the blood of the Lamb."

One of the places where my husband
preached was in the house of the man
whose wife had sold him the loaf of bread;
another was six miles up the stream, at the
post-office; and another was in a town of a
hundred inhabitants, eight miles west. In
this latter place there was but one religious
man, and he was the only physician in the
vicinity. My husband, after walking from
eight to sixteen miles and preaching three
times during the Sabbath, would sometimes
be too tired to walk home, and under such
circumstances he would sleep in the doctor's office, on the floor, using a large book
for a pillow. But quite frequently, when
the stream was frozen over or was not
too high for him to wade, he would walk
home after the evening service. Sometimes, while fording this stream, the running ice was so thick that it was both difficult and dangerous to cross.

During the winter my husband had saved
enough to purchase a cow and to partly

pay for a team. He accordingly bought a pair of horses and a wagon, and commenced to haul lumber from W—— to C——, a distance of sixty miles through an unsettled region. There were four large streams without bridges to be crossed. The load which a pair of horses could draw on the level prairie would make three loads to draw through these streams and up the steep banks; consequently, he would be delayed two hours at each of these streams. One very cold morning he had crossed the first, but, the second being larger and partly frozen over, he expected to have a hard time in getting safely to the other side with his load. But about the time he came to the stream an old man who was just moving into the country came along. He had a pair of large horses, and, seeing my husband with such a heavy load, asked him if he did not need help in crossing the stream. My husband said he did, and would be very thankful if he would as-

sist him. The old man then fastened his
horses in front of my husband's team, and
they passed through the stream without
difficulty. In like manner he helped him
over the other streams, and said it was
a pleasure to render such assistance, for
he had been in like circumstances himself.
That time my husband came home sooner
than usual, and said he hoped he could
some day recompense the old man for his
kindness. But the Lord is not unmindful
of such deeds of love to his children, nor
will he permit the doers of them to go
without reward.

Along this dreary route the prairie-wolves
—called " coyotes "—were very numerous ;
sometimes he would see them scattered
around over the prairie in large numbers.
Once they surrounded him on all sides ;
his dog was frightened, and remained under the wagon. At another time he saw a
large gray wolf but a short distance from
him ; he thought there might be others

near, and drove very fast. The wolf followed him for several miles.

But the cold winter soon passed away,
and the green grass and the beautiful flowers covered the black and charred prairie,
over which the fire had swept, burning off
the old grass; and the trees put on their
beautiful garment of green, and thus
fringed the stream which meandered
through the great meadow. The birds,
especially the lark, sang very sweetly, and
I thought it was the most beautiful country
in the world.

In the beginning of spring I went to see
my sister-friend, and she said with a smile
as I entered her cabin, "I believe I shall
get well now, for I can feel a tingle in my
fingers." All these long months she had
been more helpless than an infant, not
able to move in the least; but she was
right. She now began to improve, and
in the month of May was able to walk
out a little; soon she came to visit me,

4

and I was quite happy. I had also formed the acquaintance of another lady who became very dear to me. She had just come from Kentucky, was a good Christian, a member of the church and an active worker in the cause of the Master. Her friends had nicknamed her "Duck." I highly appreciated her frequent visits and cheerful conversation, and was always glad to see her coming to our cabin.

Now on Sunday my husband would go to his different appointments on horseback, which made the duties of the holy day more cheerful and pleasant. Instead of returning at eleven o'clock weary and with sore and wet feet, he now came back an hour earlier cheerful and happy. But he had no saddle. The people at C——, the town eight miles to the westward, said it was too bad for a man to ride on horseback so far to preach for them without any saddle, so they found and repaired an old one that had been thrown away, and one Sabbath,

after he had preached to them, they gave
him the saddle; and that old saddle did him
good service for a long time. This was the
first remuneration of an earthly kind he
had received for preaching the gospel to
these poor frontier settlers, and it might
also be considered the first real token of
their appreciation. In a short time he decided to engage wholly in the work which
he so dearly loved. A church was organized at C—— as the nucleus of a great
spiritual harvest-field. The church consisted of eleven members, and my friend
from Kentucky was one of them.

We sold one of our horses and his har-
ness, paid what we owed for the team, and
had a little left to live on until July, when
we received from the Presbyterian Board
of Home Missions our first quarter's salary,
which was one hundred and twenty-five
dollars. During this summer we continued to live in our little cabin: it was
kitchen, dining-room, parlor, bedroom and

study. My husband and oldest boy slept
on the floor. The snakes made us an occasional visit, but were not so troublesome
as they had been the summer before, as we
had ploughed around, and so had a better
chance to see them before they reached
our cabin than while we were so closely
surrounded by the dense forest of wild
blue grass and sunflower stalks. The
former in many places were eight, while
the latter were twelve, feet high.

In the autumn we concluded to move to
C——. The day we left, my dear friend
Mrs. G—— came to our cabin and said
she did not see how she could have me
leave; although she knew it was best for
us, yet she did not know what she would
do without me. We agreed to visit each
other as often as we possibly could. When
she kissed me good-bye, she bathed my
face with tears, and, while she wept to
have me go, I knew I should never have
another friend more true or dear.

About this time we received our first missionary-box. The articles were mostly new and of an excellent quality. This box came in a time of need; for, had it not been sent, we would have suffered for clothing during the winter.

CHAPTER V.

IT was in the month of October that we moved to our new home in C——. My twin-boys were a year old, and they looked so much alike that I often mistook one for the other. Real young Westerners they were, born and initiated into the rough life of the frontier. We moved into a little house with only one room, but it had a floor and was ceiled with boards, and it seemed like a palace. The rent we had to pay was eight dollars a month. Knowing that we could not live on our small salary and pay such a rent, we concluded to build a house of our own. We moved into our own home after two months, having partly paid for it. This house had two rooms and a good floor, but between my four little children and the cold winds that blew across the prairie there was only one thickness of siding. Though the winter was not so cold as the previous one had been, yet we had some storms that were very disagreeable, and on several mornings our floor was white with snow.

During the winter a great many of the poor settlers who had been there just long enough to spend all their money and not raise any crop except a little corn suffered very much. One poor Scotchman, whose wife had died and left him with a family of young children, and who lived in a dark and damp "dug-out" on the bank of the stream, was an object of pity such as is seldom seen in any country. Not only was he himself sick, but also all of his children; and, being destitute of food and clothing, their sufferings were almost beyond imagination. My husband called at

one cabin, and a man at the door told him
he did not know as he could get in, but he
might try. It was a very cold day, and he
determined to go in and get warm if he
could possibly do so. He succeeded in
getting into the cabin, but he said it was
so full that it was not without much effort
that the immates could open the door.
The cabin, he thought, was about eight
by twelve feet, and in it were an old man
and his wife and two daughters. One was
married and had a family of small children,
and it was her husband who said, "I do not
know as you can get in." That cabin had
no roof except an old wagon-sheet spread
over it, and that was full of holes; and the
wind, blowing through the walls, which were
very open, kept the old canvas fluttering
like the torn sail of a vessel in a storm.
The whole effort of the distressed ones
seemed to be to keep from freezing. The
old man said he thought if they could possibly live until spring they would be in bet-

ter circumstances by another winter. One man came to our house and said his wife had died a short time before, and he had seven young children, one a babe, and the little ones claimed his whole attention, and without assistance they would certainly perish. We divided with them at the time, and soon succeeded in gathering something for their subsistence. My husband went to see them, and said that never before had he seen such suffering humanity. The babe soon died, and the poor father said, "We shall all get through with this world soon."

The town was at this time a very rough and wicked place. Two saloons were kept blazing with quarrels and blasphemy day and night, and quite frequently a poor fellow would be sent to a drunkard's eternity without having time to say, "God be merciful to me, a sinner."

One night, very soon after dark, I sent my little boy to the post-office, and in a moment after he had left the house I heard most dreadful screams and oaths, and several shots were fired. I ran to the door and said, "Oh dear! I will not let Winnie go anywhere another night after dark;" and as I looked out I heard a ball whistle past my head. In a moment my boy came in and said, "They are having an awful fight." The next morning a young man was lying dead in a house that had been used for a meat-market. I was told that the last words he said were, "Lay me on a soft bed," but they laid him on the hard floor, and there he died.

One man who boasted of the great number of men he had killed shot a man in the Scotchman's "dug-out." The young man, who was very civil and much respected, saw the ruffian whipping a boy and told him to let the boy alone—that he was doing very wrong in whipping him. The ruffian then left the boy and told the young man he would surely kill him in-

side of a week. The young man's friends
advised him to leave the place, as the desperado had threatened to kill him and he
certainly would do so; but he said he
would not: if he was killed, it would be all
right. After three or four nights of dodging and hiding in order to keep out of the
villain's way, he went into the "dug-out"
and went to sleep. But the murderer was
on his track. In a few moments he raised
the blanket that served for a door and fired
several shots. The little children were ter-
ribly frightened and screamed, and the
young man said, "Don't shoot any more;
I am killed." The assassin then ran. The
Scotchman caught his rifle and fired at him
without effect; at the same time, one of the
children ran for the physician. The young
man reached the Scotchman some papers,
and said, "Put these into the fire; I want
to see them burn;" and after they were
burned he went out in the air and fell
down. In a moment he arose, and walked

into the dug-out in great agony and covered with perspiration. By this time the doctor came, and after examining the wound he gave him an opiate; but in one hour he was dead. The ball had passed through his lungs.

Shortly after this a well-dressed gentleman came into the town and was sitting on the counter in one of the stores, when this same desperado made his appearance in the door with revolver in hand, and said, "I wonder if I can shoot a hole through that man's hat?" The gentleman laid his hat on the counter, and said, "Yes, shoot it if you want to."—"I would rather shoot it on your head," said the ruffian.—"None of your shooting here," said the merchant; but as soon as the man put his hat on his head again he fell to the floor a dead man. The ball passed directly through his brain. The murderer mounted a fast horse and dashed off toward the timber, and in a moment was out of sight.

In a few days the town was full of strangers ; they said very little, but seemed to notice everything that was said or done. After a while a man came into town and purchased some cheese and crackers, but as he left and was crossing the stream a number of men surrounded him and put a rope around his neck, and told him he was carrying that provision to the man McCarty, who had killed so many, and if he would take them to him they would let him go, otherwise they would hang him that moment without any further ceremony. He acknowledged that the provision was for McCarty, but said that if he betrayed him the ruffian would kill him too, and he supposed he might as well die one way as another. But the strangers told him if he would take them to McCarty that was all they asked of him, and they could guarantee that he would never be harmed by the desperado. To this he consented, and in less than an hour he showed them, in a

cluster of trees, a man lying on the ground
asleep, and said, "There he is."

As the men walked toward McCarty he
heard their tramp and sprang to his feet,
and, seeing the condition he was in, ran
for his horse, which was tied to a tree a
short distance away. As many balls
whistled by his head, he turned and with
steady aim began to shoot at his assail-
ants; but ere he fired the third shot a ball
struck and shattered his wrist, and his revolver fell to the ground. He then threw
up his hands, walked up to the men, fell on
his knees and began to plead for his life.
He said he wanted at least a few days to
prepare for death before they sent him out
of the world. They said they would give
him five minutes. He said he was not fit
to die. They told him he was not fit to
live; but he crawled up to their feet and
begged for his life in a most distressing
manner, his lips quivering and tears flowing freely. When the five minutes had ex-

pired, one of the party said to a brother of the young man who had been killed in the Scotchman's dug-out, "Now is your chance: give it to him;" but the young man said he could not do it, and turned around and wept. Then several shots were heard, and the murderer's soul went into the presence of Him before whom he had hastened .the souls of so many of his fellows. His cries to man for pity instead of to God were hushed, and his body, riddled with balls, was left on the ground for the buzzards to eat. "As a man sins, so shall he be punished." The measure this ruffian had meted out to others was finally meted to him. Very brave was he until grim Death looked him in the face, and then a poor coward.

During the winter my husband held a protracted meeting in the new schoolhouse which had been built in the town, and for several nights both saloons were closed during church-time and nearly all the inhabitants of the town attended the meetings; and many of the worst and most impenitent men seemed to be very penitent. One who was considered the most hardened sinner in the town said, "This town has been run by the devil long enough, and I think it is time the people began to repent and do better." He said this in the presence of many of the wicked and profane.

It seemed as though a great revival was about to shine upon the darkness of the place, but the devil was busily at work. A small stack of hay was in dispute between two of the citizens; it was not worth more than two or three dollars. Two men attempted to take the hay; a battle followed and then a lawsuit, and nearly every one took sides with one party or the other. This strife continued until the Spirit was quenched; the light which seemed to be dawning on the place disappeared, and the meetings were given up.

CHAPTER VI.

DEATH AND DANGERS.

IT was on one cold, rainy morning in the month of March that a gentleman came to our house to tell us that Mrs. G—— was dead and her husband had sent his team for us. The dreadful news pierced my heart like an arrow. I was just anticipating a pleasant visit from her whom I loved so dearly, and to be thus so suddenly deprived of her society seemed more than I could endure.

As we rode over the prairie, which was covered with six inches of water ruffled by the strong east wind, I thought there was not a ruffle of sorrow or trouble in the cold bosom of my friend; and I almost felt a desire to bid farewell to the world, with all its cares and disappointments, and go also to the better land.

When we reached the cabin of our friends, I could scarcely enter the door to gaze upon the pale face of her who had never hung her harp on the willow because she was in a strange land. But when I looked upon the cold features, I thought there was still a smile of sweetness which the gentle spirit had left upon the clay, as the rays of the sun are seen upon the tinted clouds after it has gone down. That night I sat by the side of the fallen temple whose occupant had gone to dwell in the palace of light. I could not understand why one so lovely and so loving, so full of good deeds and so intelligent and spiritually-minded, should be called away so suddenly, while others who never threw any brightness upon the pathway of life were left to spend their days without usefulness. It seemed as though the light of the little neighborhood had been blown out. I knew she would be missed in the prayer-meeting and in the Sabbath-school, for she delighted to talk about Jesus, whom she daily worshiped. She would be missed also in many a home where her smiles and sweet conversation had so often cheered the lonely ones of her sex. Above all, she would be missed by her husband, for whose sake she had left a beautiful home and cast in her lot with the pioneers of the plains. Why did she die? Could not a physician have saved her life? "Was there no balm in Gilead, was there no physician there?" and, literally speaking, we answer, "No." The physician at C——— had gone East to die, and nearer than twenty-five miles off there was no other that could be relied on. But her time to go home had come, and she was ready. "She had fought a good fight," and then the Captain of her salvation welcomed her into the rest that remains "for the people of God."

The next day a goodly number of the people of the settlement came to pay their last respects to the departed sister. Notwithstanding the awful storm which continued to sweep over the region, by ten o'clock the little cabin was filled. My husband preached from the words, "Blessed are the dead who die in the Lord." After the sermon we laid her down by her babe in her little garden, beneath a box-elder tree which she had planted with her own hands, and as we stood around that grave and sang "Sister, thou wast mild and lovely," there were many drops falling to the ground besides those which were left there by the rain.

In less than three weeks from this time my husband preached the funeral sermons of two other ladies, who died within a mile of this place and were buried with their babes in their arms. And thus on the border hundreds of young mothers sleep beneath the cover which is red, white and blue in spring, green in summer, brown in autumn and black in winter.

The next day was the Sabbath. My husband left early in the morning to attend his different appointments, and the bereft widower went with him, leaving me alone with my little ones and God. The rain had ceased, and the sun occasionally looked down on the little mound of fresh earth beneath the cabin window. The black, heavy clouds were passing away, gradually revealing more and more of the blue sky beyond; but the clouds of sorrow were not vanishing from my poor heart. It was one of the loneliest days of my life; as with the Psalmist, tears were my meat from morning till night. My little children were out for the first flowers of the season, and sad indeed were the emotions of my soul.

> Oh the cabin so lone and drear!
> No sister there to greet;
> Her voice was music to my ear,
> Her smiles were always sweet.

In order to fulfill the requirements of the law, we again moved back to our claim, as we were in danger of losing what improvements we had made. We now built a cabin, of pine boards, twelve by fourteen feet.

One day, shortly after we moved into that little house, a thunder-storm came up suddenly from the north-west, and blew it from the foundations with such force that one corner was driven nearly a foot into the ground. Some old boxes and barrels and loose boards were hurled through the air as though they had been straws. During this storm several cabins were blown down. In one two young women were killed. Their father succeeded in getting out of the house, and hastened to remove the roof from his daughters, both of whom were dead, crushed in a shocking manner.

Here I will mention the peculiar escape of a family which happened some time before this. The cabin in which they lived was built of very small logs, and was covered with a heavy dirt roof. One night, after a storm, the whole family were seated around the fireplace, which was one of the old-fashioned kind, built on the outside of the house, so that it was not covered by the dirt roof. It was late in the evening, and the fire had burned nearly out, when they were startled by a sudden crash, at the sound of which they all sprang into the fireplace. They had probably before thought of adopting this plan, and it proved to be successful, for they all escaped uninjured. As the roof fell in the walls fell out.

In the following July, Indian troubles commenced anew. For several days we had heard of the atrocious deeds of the savages. We knew that several tribes were on the war-path, and that serious troubles were inevitable.

On Sunday night my husband returned home very late; he had preached three times and had ridden on his pony nearly thirty miles, and was very weary. He said he thought he should fall from his saddle before he could reach home. We soon retired, and in a short time were fast asleep. About two in the morning we were startled by a loud rap on the door. Two of our neighbors called my husband out, so that the children and myself should not be frightened, and told him some of our neighbors had been killed and scalped, and that his family was the only one left in the neighborhood. The men had their rifles in their hands, and seemed to be much excited and in a great hurry; so they hastened away, telling my husband to look out for himself and his family. We did not sleep any more that night. We had no horses, and the night was dark; so we could only pray for God to protect us and our four small children, and wait for the morning light.

Before coming to the West I had often

read of those who lived in constant dread
of the arrow and the scalping-knife, and
many a time I thought I could tell something about how they felt; but now I
learned that imagination was not reality.
Neither were dangers far away like dangers near at hand. The reading of these
things was like the distant thunder when
not a cloud could be seen, but now the
heavens were black and the thunderbolt
seemed to be striking at my feet. The still-
ness of the night, only occasionally broken
by the distant howling of wolves or by the
barking of a dog, and the thought that the
treacherous red men might be stealthily
creeping through the awful darkness, and
that at any moment we might be surprised
by their horrid yells, made the lingering
hours of darkness dismal almost beyond
endurance. We felt powerless; we had
no weapons of defence except an axe,
and our little house, being built of pine,
would burn like a torch. But after this

awful night of suspense we were cheered by the morning light.

Old frontiersmen had told us that Indians often made their attack very early in the morning, and in a few moments two men (not those who came in the night) who were living in a log house a short distance away came to our cabin and said the Indians were coming, and advised us to take our children to their house, saying that they would defend us, as they were well armed. We had no time to lose, as the Indians were so near that we could see their red blankets, and were riding very fast; but we were scarcely in the cabin before they turned and rode off in another direction. The house to which we fled for refuge was built of hewed logs, and the Indians are generally very cautious in making an attack upon such houses, from which many of them have been killed by shots fired at them between the logs of the walls.

The Attack of the Indians.   Page 74.

By this time the excitement had become
so great that few men dared to remain to
take care of and defend their property.
The men who said they would defend us
now concluded to leave, and they kindly
offered to take myself and my children
with them to a place of safety. My husband resolved to remain and take care of
our little home and the homes of others
who had left the place.

Shortly before night we came to a place
on the bank of a small stream where hundreds of men, women and children who
were on the retreat had stopped for the
night; and here we concluded to take our
chance with the crowd. But few of them
were armed, and it seemed to us as though
"the sheep were gathered together for the
slaughter." About the middle of the night
a man came riding up in haste, and said
there were more than a thousand Indians
not five miles away and coming directly
toward the spot. This caused an alarm-

ing stampede. The shrieks and cries of the women and the children made the scene more dismal. In a few moments every man, woman and child had left the place; and if ever wheels flew across the prairie, they did then.

I shall never forget one man who had an ox-team. His wagon was old and the tires on the wheels were loose, and his precious load consisted of his wife and children. That poor man, with whip in one hand, which he used briskly on the oxen, and a stone in the other hand, which he used to keep the tires from coming off the wheels, ran about twelve miles, striking the oxen with one hand and the wheels with the other. He died a short time after, and I believe this night hastened his death.

Whether or not there was any truth in the report that the Indians were so near I could never learn, but I always thought it was much exaggerated.

The next day I arrived with my children

at a village forty miles from our home,
where I remained a few days; but, as the
people there were much excited and
alarmed, I resolved to go back to my
home.

When I returned, my husband's face was
bruised and swollen. He said that the
night before he had gone into a cabin to
stay with some young men who were keeping cattle and horses; the night was very
warm, and they lay down leaving the door
open. He thought, before he went to sleep,
"Perhaps the red men may use their toma-
hawks on our heads before morning;" but
instead of an Indian's tomahawk, a large
deer's horn which was hanging up in the
room fell and struck him in the face. He
said that for several minutes he thought he
had been struck by an Indian.

The night I arrived at home we tied our
horse close to the door, and I concluded to
have one night's rest even if I should never
have another. But in the night I received

a fright that I did not get over for several days. Something pushed against the door with such force that the windows rattled and the whole house shook. My husband sprang from the bed, caught the axe and opened the door. It was the horse rubbing himself.

After this we slept for several nights in the corn-field, and many a restless and weary hour did I spend in that field of corn. One night I did not close my eyes in sleep; I heard noises like the tramping of horses and the rustling of corn, and I knew I could see dark forms moving by at times. My clothing was wet with perspiration from within and the heavy night-dew from without. Morning revealed the fact that some horses had jumped out of the pasture and made their way into our field.

A short time after this the great scare began to abate; a good many soldiers were sent into the place, and all signs of Indians disappeared. The soldiers remained about a month. A few of them spent much of their time visiting among the settlers. One of them called at a dug-out in which lived a very large family (ten children, besides the parents). This soldier took a seat on the bed, but a sharp cry caused him to spring to his feet: he had sat down on a baby. He excused himself as the mother endeavored to pacify the little one, and in a moment seated himself at the other end of the bed, when another cry was heard. He then took his hat and left, declaring it was the most prolific country in the world. The woman had twin-babes, and had laid one at each end of the bed.

CHAPTER VII.

WHAT LIQUOR DOES.

ALTHOUGH the great excitement began to die away, yet apprehensions of danger were still felt by many. Some said the Indians were waiting for the settlers to become quiet and feel secure, and then they would make a raid into the settlement and kill and scalp to their hearts' content. This thought caused constant dread and uneasiness.

About this time my husband went to town, and as he rode along the main street a lady at the hotel came out and told him that the shoemaker had just been killed and the murderer had asked to see him. She also said they would hang the man who had committed the crime, and that he wanted to see him as soon as possible. My husband sprang from his horse, and first ran into the shop to see if the shoemaker was really dead, and there he lay, cold and silent, by the side of his bench. He then hastened to the cabin to see the murderer, and to his surprise he found a young man, about eighteen years of age, with smooth feminine features and well dressed. His hands were tied together, also his feet. My husband asked him why he had committed such a dreadful deed. The young man said he did not intend to kill the shoemaker, but only to scare him, and that he was sorry, and asked my husband to pray for him; at the same time he told my husband that he was a church-member and had been brought up by religious parents. My husband then prayed for him. The murderer also prayed for God to have mercy upon his poor lost soul, crying very earnestly for the Lord to save him. Al-

6

though the night was cold, the young man was in such agony that large drops of sweat kept constantly trickling down his face and neck, and he continued to pray to God for mercy.

During the first of the evening there was quite a crowd in and around the cabin ; it was in the midst of this crowd of wicked men that my husband prayed and conversed with the murderer about his soul's salvation. About ten o'clock the crowd began to disappear, and by eleven they were all gone except one man, who was left as a guard. Occasionally a man would come and look in at the door. The prisoner begged my husband to remain until morning, feeling confident that the minister's presence would save his life, —at least, for that night.

At midnight all was quiet. The prisoner was seated on a block, and a large rough man was standing by his side with a revolver in his hand; in one corner of the room, burning faintly, was a candle, which flickered as the wind blew through the open walls. A few dim lights could be seen on the distant prairie, and one still lingered in the office of the hotel. The night was dark; not a star was to be seen. The prisoner said he was reconciled and not afraid to die. The guard promised to protect him if he could; and after advising him to look to Jesus, who himself died on a tree, my husband left him, mounted his horse and started for home.

That night, before the sun went down, I had looked a great many times over the hazy prairie to see if my husband was coming. His horse was white, and I could discern it a long distance away; but I looked and looked in vain until I could no longer distinguish objects on the plains, and then I took my seat by the cabin window, stared through the darkness and listened until after twelve for the familiar tramp of the horse's feet, but no white

horse could I see. Several times I imagined I could hear the sound of the horse's
feet, but it would soon die away in the distance, and all would be silent.

I waited some time after twelve o'clock,
and then I resolved to leave the children
in bed and go in search of my husband;
for I knew that something serious had
happened to him or to some one else, for
about that time he was prompt in returning
home before dark, unless some of our neighbors' wives or daughters were with me. I
thought of several things that might have
detained him, but my great fear was that
a party of red men had detected his white
horse and killed and scalped him as they
had some of our neighbors. But I had
gone only a short distance before I heard
the quick click of a horse's feet. Can it be
my husband, or is it a party of Indians? was
my thought. I stepped out of the path
into a little ravine and watched until I
could see the white horse; and when I

called, my husband was startled to find me so far from the cabin. The next morning the young man was hanging to a limb of a cottonwood tree.

If I should be asked what was the cause of this terrible affair, my answer would be, " Whisky." The day before the murder the shoemaker was intoxicated and used unbecoming language to some ladies at the hotel. This young man put him out of the house and whipped him, and was praised by the ladies, who said he did a good deed. The next day the young man was drinking. He had heard frontiersmen talk about shooting, and, with his brain fired with liquor, he concluded to show his bravery by killing some one. Although he told my husband he did not intend to kill the man, a boy at the hotel said that the murderer, while loading his revolver, had told him that the shoemaker had only five minutes to live. He doubtless intended to kill him, and thought it would be considered a brave and noble act; which would have been the case had he committed the deed in self-defence. But it was premeditated murder. As he went into the shop the shoemaker raised his hand and said, "Don't shoot!" but the words were no sooner spoken than he fell from his bench, and in a moment he was dead.

A few days after this the murderer's father, an old man with white locks, came into the town and asked a boy to go with him to the cemetery and show him the grave of his son. The old man spent several hours by that grave weeping, and after he had written his son's name on a flat stone and stood it at the head of the grave he walked away, and passed out of the town weeping and sobbing as though his aged heart would break.

About this time the grasshoppers came down upon us. The air was darkened, and in a short time after they commenced to fall I could not find room for the sole of

my foot on the ground without crushing
vast numbers of them. The roof, and also
the walls, of our cabin were covered, and
our windows were darkened. The roar of
their wings was like the sound of distant
and continued thunder. In less than three
days nearly every green thing had disappeared: they devoured even the leaves of
the trees. I had experienced terrible storms
of sand and dust, but I had never seen
such a storm of living creatures before.
They swirled in the air, and came down
"heaps upon heaps" until the very earth
seemed to throb with life. The corn was
destroyed, and the little fruit trees were
eaten nearly to the ground. This trouble,
in addition to the other calamities, so completely discouraged the people that hundreds left their improvements and fled
from that region; but such as had no
horses or money were compelled to remain, let the consequence be what it
would.

About this time we moved back to
C——. As a sick woman was occupying
our house, we rented an old box shanty
which stood between the two saloons.
During the time we lived in this house
I experienced more of the horrors of
strong drink than I had ever before imagined could exist anywhere on this fair
earth of ours.   A thin board partition,
which had been perforated with balls and
shot, separated our room from one of the
dens of vice, which I could not conceive of
being surpassed in iniquity and degradation by the "bottomless pit" itself.   I need
not mention the awful stench—which it was
not difficult to imagine as coming from the
lower regions—the bitter oaths and obscene
language or the shriek and racket as a poor
fellow would be felled to the floor when
struck on the head by perhaps a brother
or a friend; neither need I mention the
clatter of broken bottles as the glass would
fall to the floor or the mournful and sud-

den cries and unintelligible expressions of such as suffered with delirium tremens; for all these are the offspring of Bacchus, the outgrowth of such places of death, and branches of the parent stock.

One man in this saloon was dying with delirium tremens. My husband had known him when he was a sober and respectable man, but a few months were sufficient to complete the sad story: he embraced the boisterous society of that saloon instead of giving his heart to the Saviour; and there he drank, and there he died. While my husband conversed with him before he passed away he cried out in his wandering thoughts, "I'll go to church when I get well." A number of his old associates promised to take care of him until morning; but in the morning he was dead, and his companions in sin, who had promised to watch over him, were all asleep on the floor: he died alone. They brought in a rough box, and one took him by the feet and

the other by the hair of his head, and
they dropped him into that box as though
he had been a dead dog.

How true are the words, " The wages of
sin is death "! and how little mercy for one
another dwells in the hearts of bad men
whose ways please not God !

As my health was poor, a young friend
came to stay with me for a few weeks. One
night after she came a terrible uproar was
heard in the saloon ; in a moment a crowd
gathered in front of our door, and in the
midst of horrid yells and curses the crack-
ing of pistols commenced. The young lady
screamed and wanted to leave the house,
for she said we should all be killed before
morning. It was a scene to try the strong-
est nerves—the constant flash of firearms
streaming by the window, accompanied
with hoarse voices uttering threats and
blasphemous oaths—but the crowd soon
dispersed ; and, strange to say, no one
was killed, though several were injured.

I think it was the next night that a number of herders were becoming very merry, when I heard some one say, "Boys, boys, keep still! The preacher lives in there."—"Is that so?" said one. "My father also is a preacher." Thenceforward things were more quiet until we moved into our own house, and then there was a grand rejoicing. We moved about dark, and as soon as we left the young people began to gather in the shanty to have a dance; and in a short time the vacated room was lighted brightly and the revel began. One of our church-members, who always claimed that it was no harm to dance, heard the noise, and, not knowing that we had moved, hastened home and told his wife he would never go to hear that minister preach again. "Why?" asked his wife, much surprised. Her husband replied, "His house is full, and they are playing the fiddle and dancing."—"Why, Mr. T——, you are certainly mistaken!"—"I am not mistaken. I was

particular to look in, and saw them with
my own eyes." The wife then said she
would go and see for herself; so she and
her sister went out to convince themselves,
and they said they would have to believe it.
Then they went home, and in a few minutes a very wicked and profane man came
in, and was told that the preacher was
having a dance at his house. "That is
no more than I should have expected,"
said the scoffer; "these preachers are always telling others not to do the very
things they do themselves. But really I
do not think it is any more harm for a
preacher to dance than it is for any other
church-member."—"I do," said Mr. T——;
"I think a preacher should set a good
example." The young man replied that
if it was a sin for one of Christ's followers
to dance, it was a sin for another, preacher or no preacher; but if it was no sin, he
thought a minister should not be censured
for dancing or allowing others to dance

in his house. But Mr. T—— and his wife
and sister said that they thought less of
the preacher and his wife, and felt as though
they would never go to another dance as
long as they lived.

Early the next morning, as I looked
out of the window of my home, I saw
this woman go to the house from which
we had moved. After rapping two or
three times she looked in, and, finding
no one there, she came directly to our
door. As I opened it and said, "Good-
morning, Mrs. T——," she came in laughing and told me the whole story, and said
she never before realized how dreadful it
would seem for a minister to have a crowd
of rough, wicked people in his house dancing, and she had concluded to attend no
more dances. I told her that to a minister
it seemed as bad to see the members of
his church dancing as it did to them to
see him dancing. She replied that she had
never thought of it in that way before.

CHAPTER VIII.

THE PENALTY OF HORSE-STEALING.

ABOUT this time, one morning very early, before the sun had thrown his golden light over the grassy plains, I looked out of the window and saw armed men coming into the town from every direction. I told my husband that the Indians were certainly near, otherwise there would not be so many armed men around the town so early in the morning. He went out, but soon returned, telling me that the sheriff was in town and had arrested several men for stealing horses. And here let me give a brief description of the men who were arrested.

First, Mr. M———, a man of some property, lived in a neat log house one mile from town; he was a large fleshy man, but crippled with rheumatism. He had kept a dance-house, but it was burned by the citizens, and he had barely escaped with his life. This morning, as the sheriff went into his house, his wife said her husband was sick; but the sheriff with his men took him out of his bed, saying that he must go to W——, sick or well.

Second, Mr. T——, a saloon-keeper whose wife was a Catholic. My husband called at their house a short time before this, and she told him that he had better not call again, as her husband did not like preachers, although they both came to hear him preach quite frequently.

Third, Mr. C——, a hotel-keeper, a very bad man; his wife was a very bad woman. Both drank whisky and used profane language, and quarreled constantly, not only with each other, but also with their neighbors.

Fourth, Mr. H——, a young lawyer,

about twenty-two years of age, and considered the most handsome young man in that country. He had been educated in the city of New York, and not only had more than usual ability as an attorney, but possessed those qualities which are requisite in any young man in order to make him a gentleman of the first class. But he was not a good man; he kept bad company and spent more money than he could honorably earn, and seemed to sink gradually into those sins by which the hopes and the prospects of thousands of young men are blasted for time and eternity. A short time before this my husband roomed with him one night; he seemed very amiable, but did not want to talk on the subject of religion.

Fifth, Mr. S——, said to have been the son of an ex-governor, but very much degraded on account of strong drink; his right arm had been amputated at the shoulder, so that he could do but little work of any kind. During the previous winter he sat day after day in front of the saloons dressed in the same old brown suit; his hair was long and matted; he slept wherever night found him—in the stable, on the saloon floor, and doubtless many a time on the cold ground. He was so completely under the influence of whisky, and so thoroughly controlled by bad men, that he would not listen to any words of friendly counsel from those who would gladly have befriended him. My husband endeavored to encourage him to do right, but with profane language he railed at him and refused to be admonished. After this, when he was more sober, my husband attempted to counsel him again. This time he did not seem to be altogether void of feeling; tears came to his eyes, and a few nights after this we saw him at church for the first time, and, notwithstanding the degradation into which vice had plunged him, we thought there was some prospect of his

7

reformation.   But, instead of yielding his
heart to the Saviour at once, he continued
to embrace his fetters and kiss the chains
that held him, soul and body, to the slow
but unquenchable fires of vice.

Sixth, Mr. B——. He had lived at
C—— but a short time, and was doubtless a bad man; he was very large, and
about thirty years of age. The day before
the arrest he was in the town with a rifle
looking for another desperado that he might
kill him; at the same time the other was
lurking around and dodging from place to
place, seeking an opportunity to kill Mr.
B——. He lived in a dug-out, half a mile
from town. When the sheriff and his men
rode up, Mr. B—— at first refused to allow
himself to be taken, and the following conversation took place:

Sheriff. Come out and give yourself up
like a man.

B. You will never take me alive.

S. If you will give yourself up, I will

defena you from the mob and you shall have a fair trial.

B. I should never get to W—— alive.

S. I have control of my men; and if you will give yourself up, I pledge my word that you shall have a fair trial.

B. I know the mob will hang me, and I will not give myself up alive. If you take me, you will take me a dead man; but I will sell my life as dearly as possible.

S. I will give you ten minutes to send your wife out of the dug-out.

B. My wife will assist me; so proceed as soon as you like.

S. Send your wife out, and we will let her depart in peace. I do not wish to fight a woman.

B. My wife will not leave; she is a better warrior than you or any of the men you have in your crowd.

S. You are foolish to lose your own life and endanger the life of your wife rather than defend yourself before an honorable court, with the probability of being set at liberty.

B. I am not afraid of an honorable court, but I understand mob-law too well to expect any such thing as that should I give myself up as a prisoner to-day ; so I shall not throw myself into the hands of a mob. But I do not object to dying here. I have the advantage, and will sell my life as dearly as possible.

S. I have two hundred men, and it will not take long to bring you out.

B. I know that, but you will exchange a good many lives for mine. I am all ready; so go right ahead without any more talk.

Mrs. B—— was small in stature, with pale and delicate features, large bright eyes and short curly hair. She had listened to the above conversation without a shudder. She had great confidence in herself, as well as in her husband, and she doubtless thought that within the fort they could cope with the whole crowd. As the sheriff was conversing with the men, she said in a low but unfaltering tone, " Will, be firm. I will stand by you to the last. We will either conquer or die together." As she said this she lifted a revolver in one hand and held a knife in the other, firmly grasped; nor did her slender hands tremble. At this time another voice called out to Mr. B—— (it was that of an old acquaintance) and said, " You are perfectly safe in surrendering; the sheriff tells me there is no danger. I will go with you to W—— and see that you are not harmed;" and upon this Mr. B—— surrendered, disregarding the most earnest entreaties of his wife.

About the middle of the day the sheriff, with his six prisoners and the posse whom he had deputized, left C—— for W——. My husband, understanding the storm that was brewing, concluded to follow the prisoners and befriend them as much as he possibly could. He said he felt very guilty

to think he had not been more in earnest
in seeking the salvation of those poor unfortunate fellows, who had souls to be saved
or lost, and he concluded to make another
effort to bring them, like the poor one who
died at Jesus' side, within the everlasting
arms of love.   But, alas! how suddenly
and awfully are our opportunities for usefulness cut off!

He arrived in W—— as the sun was setting; the prisoners were there in the calaboose. The town was full of men, and all
seemed to be much excited. My husband
had often preached in W——, and was
acquainted with many of the citizens, and
with most of the people through the country, for he had conversed with them at their
own firesides, and he thought he might intercede successfully for the prisoners. He
was told that they would certainly be
lynched before morning. He then concluded to see the sheriff and obtain permission to spend the night with them. He

desired to pray and converse with them, and to save their lives if possible. He accordingly went to the sheriff's house and asked permission to enter the calaboose and converse with the men who, he believed, would never see the light of another morning. But the sheriff said, "Not to-night; you may go in the morning," and then went out. His wife added that she feared it would be too late by that time.

As my husband left the place an old friend met him and said, "You must be careful what you say here to-night. It won't do for you to say anything in favor of those men; you know a great many of our people have lost their horses, and intense excitement prevails." My husband replied that a crowd of two or three hundred could not be collected without a large part of the men being persons known to him, and he would venture at least to intercede for the prisoners. His friend said he knew it was not safe, for there would be hundreds and most of them would be under the influence of whisky, and in such circumstances men were very different from what they might seem to a minister in their own homes.

These words, from a man of excellent judgment and a very dear friend, had much force with my husband; yet still he determined to seek an opportunity to talk with the wretched criminals in the calaboose. His friend told him that his wife would like to see him, and asked him to come to his house; and as soon as they had entered, the man locked the door and told my husband that he should not go out again that night. The sheriff had refused to let him see the prisoners, and a friend at whose house he had often found a welcome home had, on account of an interest in his personal safety, locked the door and said he must not go out; so he retired to his room to spend the night in prayer.

It was a beautiful evening. The moon shone brightly; scarcely a cloud could be seen, and a gentle south-west breeze added to the enjoyment of such as were seeking recreation by walking in the flowery paths that surrounded the village. But about the middle of the night, as he looked out upon the loveliness of nature, he heard the heavy tramp of many feet, and could see groups of men moving quickly along the streets. He then prayed to God to have mercy upon the souls about to leave the bodies of clay and go into his presence, and to forgive their sins as well as his own negligence in not being more faithful in the discharge of his duty.

When the morning dawned he walked out, and the calaboose door was open; he went down to the stream, and as he was crossing the bridge he saw three forms, the bodies of H——, S—— and B——, suspended to an oak-limb which reached out over the old road that led up from the stream and was traveled before the bridge was built. H——, the lawyer, was near the end of the limb, and perhaps twenty feet from the ground. His feet were swaying to and fro, and his brown hair, streaming in the wind, occasionally fell over his purple forehead. Next to him was the body of the man with only one arm, dressed in the same old brown jacket and overalls that he wore the previous winter while sitting in front of the saloons, and near the trunk of the tree was the body of Mr. B——, whom the sheriff allowed to fall into the clutches of a drunken mob, to be murdered by the hands of lawless men, many of whom were doubtless more guilty than himself.

The bodies were taken down and laid in the court-house, and my husband was standing there as Mrs. B—— came in. She had followed her husband twenty-five miles on foot, and she fell down on the floor by his side and wept as though her heart was

ready to burst with grief. The sheriff
turned to my husband, saying,

"This is pretty rough."

"Yes," was the reply; "hundreds to kill
their poor unfortunate brothers, but few to
take them by the hand and with kind words
encourage them to do better and become
honorable men."

Mrs. B—— bought a coffin for her husband and gave him a decent burial. The
others were put in rough boxes and taken
to the cemetery, followed by no friends to
weep over their remains.

After the men were incarcerated they
sent for two very able and popular law-
yers, who told the prisoners that if they
would pay them one hundred dollars each
they would set them at liberty. M——,
T—— and C—— were able to raise the
amount, and so escaped; the others were
left to their fate.

As they put the rope around the lawyer's
neck he said he felt faint and asked for some

water, and they went to the stream and brought him some in a hat. He drank, and then said, "Boys, let me go, and I will leave the place and never return ; you will never hear of me again." Some hearts were touched ; others cried, "No!" He then said, "My life is of no account, but don't ever let my parents know what became of me : it would break their hearts."

It is true that many of the people had lost their horses, and this was considered the most effectual means of putting an end to the stealing; which proved true, for after this there was not a horse stolen in the vicinity for more than a year. But it is an awful remedy to take men, with no certainty as to their guilt, and hang them like dogs, without even time or opportunity to repent of their evil deeds.

In this case we have always thought that the guilty ones escaped and the innocent (as to the crime of which they were ac-

cused) suffered. My husband preached
against this kind of proceeding, and said
it was murder; and he was asked by several men at the close of different meetings
if he thought there was any forgiveness for
a man who had taken the life of a fellow-
mortal. One man who assisted in this
work of death was a praying man. A
short time after this he said that he saw
the one whom he had tied come into his
room in the night, and, being a supersti-
tious man, he was so worried that he left
the place. I have no doubt that many of
those engaged in this violence have seriously repented before this. Had the pro-
fessed Christians of that mob endeavored
as earnestly to bring these wicked men to
the Saviour as they did to send them out of
the world, they might to-day have been
happy Christians, rejoicing with those who
showed them the way. But it is so easy
to do wrong, and so hard to do right!

CHAPTER IX.

A HARD WINTER.

DURING the following winter the suffering of the poor settlers was more severe than in the previous winter. Crops had been almost a failure, and the excitement caused by the Indians had so interfered with the labors of the people that many who would have had comfortable houses were compelled to live in hovels or in dug-outs. The cry of distress was heard by the benevolent of almost every State in the Union, and valuable aid in the shape of boxes of clothing, provisions and money was sent for the relief of the sufferers.

But, on account of the many drainings of selfishness on either side, the stream of charity became very small by the time it reached the extreme border. Men who were in good circumstances grasped more eagerly for the aid sent to the sufferers than did the actually destitute and needy. A car-load of corn was shipped to the nearest railroad station, to be divided among the needy ones of our country, and to be used only for seed. One man who had a hundred head of cattle, a hundred acres sown to wheat, and several horses, also land and money, took one of his independent neighbors with him, and the two managed to secure all the corn for themselves; so that the poor and suffering ones never received a kernel of it, to my knowledge.

The frontier, where men and women are separated from those influences by which they were surrounded before leaving their homes in the East, and living among strangers far away on the plains, is one of the best places in the world to study human nature and to learn the utter de-

pravity of mankind. Here the passions
of avarice, lust and oppression are not re-
strained by public sentiment. The hyp-
ocrite reveals himself in his true light.
Here is seen the cloven foot of the beast,
the fangs of the serpent and the poison of
the adder. Many a father would blush
with shame if he knew the disgraceful
deeds committed by his once seemingly
noble boy. Many a mother would weep
tears of anguish could she know the depths
of wretchedness into which her daughter
has fallen. Many a school-teacher would
be astonished if he knew how the bright
boy and the beautiful girl who were once
ornaments in his school are now living in
the West. Many a pastor would be greatly
humbled, and would feel as did the proph-
et when he cried out "How is the gold
become dim! How is the most fine gold
changed!" if he knew the conduct of the
man whom he once thought to be almost
a saint.

It is an actual fact that many died for the want of the very assistance intended for them, but which was snatched away from their mouths by the greedy hands of selfishness.

During this winter my husband preached but little. In the autumn he contracted a heavy cold, which finally settled in his eyes, causing him much pain and comparative blindness until the next spring. Our house was still unplastered, having only the siding between my five children and the cold prairie storms. With my afflicted husband, and people constantly coming, I endured the winter as one of extreme toil and anxiety. Our meetings were well attended during the autumn, until my husband's eyes became so inflamed and painful that he was compelled to give up the work. He had just commenced a protracted meeting, and I have no doubt that the anxiety which he had for Christ's cause in that dark land, with much study

8

and reading at night and going from hot
rooms so often out in the cold air, were
the main causes of his sad affliction.

One very cold morning, about the time
he gave up his ministerial work on account
of his eyes, the aged man who helped him
over the streams when he was hauling lumber came into town with a load of wood
to exchange for provisions. After unload-
ing it at the hotel he came into our house
to get warm. As he drew his chair close
to the fire and shivered, he said he could
not face the cold storms as he could once.
He wore an old brown hat tied under his
chin; on his jacket patch had been added
to patch until the original had nearly disappeared. As he sat by the fire there ran
from his eye down over his withered cheek
a tear, the track of which he wiped away
with his rough hand. My husband, re-
membering the kindness of the old man
when first they met as strangers, now felt
greatly stimulated to repay him. He ac-

cordingly pulled off his coat and told Mr.
A—— to put it on ; the old man hesitated
a moment, and then did so. He then gave
the old man an overcoat, which he took
from a box that had been sent for the
poor, and he put that on also ; and when
he left the house, he was not only warm
and comfortable, but very thankful and
happy.

This winter was the hardest on the poor
settlers of any we had experienced. As the
spring came again thousands hailed it with
joy and gladness, and the little children
went forth from their home prisons to
gather beautiful flowers, to play in the
running streams, and to enjoy the sweet
breezes that breathed so musically through
the tree-tops, where the birds were singing
and the buds bursting.

It was early in the month of May my
friend "Duck" came to visit me. I was
alarmed to see how poor and pale she was.
She said she had been "real sick." Her

husband was herding cattle out on the
plains. They had no children. She was
a brave woman—had fought the wolves
in front of her cabin door, had traveled
around with her husband on horseback,
and had learned much of the nomadic life
of the plains. She had been with me only
a short time before I concluded, judging
from the hollow cough, the sunken eye—
which had lost its natural lustre—the pale
features and the quick pulse, that she was
a consumptive. I told her she must remain a while with me, and I would take
care of her. But, instead of improving,
she continued to fail very fast until the
middle of June, when it became evident
to her as well as to her friends that her
days in this world were few. Her husband was sent for; he seemed much af-
fected to find his wife so low. He sent
sixty miles for a physician, who gave him
no encouragement. She continued to get
weaker until the eighth day of July, when

she peacefully crossed over the dark river. Before she passed away she conversed with me about the love of Jesus and her willingness to trust him, but said she was so sorry for her poor husband. And thus joined the heavenly company one of whom it could well have been said,

"None knew her but to love her,
    None named her but to praise."

During the spring we built to our house an addition which we intended for two bedrooms, but at this time a quilt answered for a partition. About a week before my friend died, my husband was taken sick with malarial fever, and was now very low. He was not able to attend the funeral. Mr. C——, the widower, said he could not have his wife buried without a sermon. My husband told him of a minister twenty-five miles away, who was the nearest clergyman of any evangelical Church. This minister was sent for, and conducted the funeral

services. Before Mrs. C—— died she wanted me by her side nearly all the time. With
her in one room and my sick husband in the
other, and all my little children to look after
and care for, my strength failed, and as soon
as she breathed her last I was prostrate and
not able to do any work for nearly two
weeks, at which time my husband was so
reduced that our neighbors said he would
be the next to be carried from that town
to the cemetery. But God willed it otherwise; he has lived to see laid in their graves
many of those who were then strong and
healthy.

At that time our friends were very kind,
and we were well cared for; but as we began to recover we found our financial circumstances very embarrassing. Our doctor's bills had broken in heavily upon our
small income, and it was only by very strict
economy and pinching that we were enabled to pay our debts and keep our credit
good. We had two cows, but before this

they both died. Our salary was five hundred dollars from the Board of Home Missions, and we did not receive as much from the people with whom we were laboring as we gave to the sufferers, for we were constantly dividing with those who were more needy than ourselves.

A family consisting of husband, wife and twelve children lived in a little shanty near the town. They were very destitute. One day I went to their place. Some of the little ones were out playing without any clothing on; they were as brown as buns. The mother said it was impossible to keep them clothed. I filled a pillow-case with such articles as I could spare, and gave it to her. A short time after this the eldest girl (and eldest child) married our baker. He was a stirring young man, and by hard work and economy had been able to purchase a few groceries to sell in connection with his bakery. His property, including his house and lot, could not have been

sold for more than five hundred dollars;
but the young and foolish girl thought
she had married the richest man in all
the country. The baker soon found that
he had married not only the girl, but the
whole of her family; for he had them all
to maintain, which soon caused serious
trouble.

My husband called on one family and
asked the woman to come to church and
Sabbath-school with her children. She said
they were too poor and had no clothing
good enough to wear. "Well," said he,
"mend and put on the best you have;
do your duty and worship God, and perhaps you will have better after a while."
—"Yes," replied the old lady; "the Bible
says, 'Patch up your old coat and wear it
until you are able to buy a new one,'" and
said she knew she was not mistaken, for
she had read it in the Bible many a time.
He advised her to obey that command, but
she did not. Such is the ignorance con-

cerning the Bible which prevails among a certain class on the border.

In the autumn my husband went out with a party to hunt buffaloes. After one day's drive there came up a fearful storm, and they all remained under their wagon-covers and shivered, while the poor horses shivered standing by the wagons. The storm lasted nearly twenty-four hours, and the prairie was flooded and the streams in the ravines were so swollen as to make the attempt to cross them very unsafe. But they were soon enabled to travel by keeping on the highest ground. In a short time, as they passed over a little hill, they found themselves within a few rods of an Indian village. The Indians saw them and came streaming out of their wigwams and surrounded them on every side. Some had bows and arrows, some had rifles and others had knives. My husband said that for a moment he thought his time had come to die. But one of the party had been an

Indian-trader, and the Indians knew him. The chief spoke a few words to his braves, and they laid down their arms. A negro was among the party of hunters, and some of the young Indians seemed determined to have his scalp. They gathered around him with long sharp knives, and would probably have scalped him had not the chief interfered. The Indians soon went back to their wigwams, and the hunters were permitted to go along unmolested. The poor negro, however, kept feeling the top of his head, and continued to groan until the next morning. A few days after this a party of hunters were actually killed and scalped near this place.

The next day the hunting-party went out in the morning, leaving my husband to take care of the stuff and prepare dinner. In a short time a large brown bear came around the side of one of the hills, walked close to the camp and stood on his hind feet, and there remained for near-

ly a half hour. My husband did not have
a gun, or even an axe: the party had taken
all the arms with them. He knew it would
be useless to run; so he stood and watched
the bear, and the bear watched him. After
getting tired, Bruin dropped down on his
fore feet and walked back slowly behind
the hill. My husband then went and found
the rest of the party, about a mile away.
They had killed a buffalo, and were bringing in some of the meat for dinner. They
moved to another camping-place, and concluded to let the bear alone, if he should
not be the first aggressor.

Another hunting-party were out about
fifty miles from home; they had been very
successful, had their wagons loaded with
choice buffalo meat and hides, antelopes
and turkeys, and intended to start for
home in the morning. As they had seen
no signs of Indians, they were careless and
neglected to keep a guard; and in the
morning one of their wagon-wheels was

gone, a prop had been put under the axle-tree to support the load and the wheel had been taken away. This left the party in a bad condition, as the others would not go away and leave their comrade in distress.

In this situation they remained until about ten o'clock, not knowing what to do. Finally a party of six Indians came in sight, and rode slowly along as if they were going in another direction, but concluded to call and see what was the difficulty with the hunters. As they came up one of the party approached them, and told them of their bad condition. The Indians said they would get the wheel and bring it to them if each of the party would pay them two dollars; to this the hunters agreed, and in less than three hours they came with the wheel. They put a stick through the hub, and two were rolling it along through the grass. They said they took it from another tribe. The hunters knew they had taken it themselves, but they paid them according to contract, and were very glad to get the wheel back at such a low price. The Indians divided the money and rode off, and the party rolled out for home and did not give the red men a chance to steal another of their wheels.

CHAPTER X.

BRIDAL AND DEATH.

THIS summer the crops were good. Wheat averaged nearly twenty bush-els to the acre, corn about forty, and oats fifty. Vegetables were an excellent yield, and all the poor settlers could indulge freely in the luxury of watermelons. The people were now greatly encouraged; real estate rose fifty per cent. in value. Immi-gration began to pour into the place, and better times were not only anticipated, but experienced by all.

About this time my husband said I could have all his marriage fees to purchase such articles as I needed in the house. Some of the newly-married grooms were quite liberal, but among the rest of the happy couples there came a young man and a young lady to be married. I brushed up the lady's clothing and assisted her in getting ready, called in some of our friends, and after the ceremony prepared dinner for all, expecting to be remunerated with a five-dollar bill ; but the young lady had lived near us before we moved to C——, and one day, while she was visiting at our house, we were speaking of a friend who was just married, and my husband said to her, " If you will get married, I will marry you for nothing ;" so now she said she should hold him to his promise, and they never gave us a cent.

Another man asked, after the ceremony, " How much do you charge for marrying people ?" My husband said he made no charge ; but, as the young man continued to insist on knowing the amount of his bill, he said the law allowed a justice of the peace three dollars. " Three dollars for a little job that can be done in ten

minutes!" said the newly-married man.—
"Give me what you think it is worth," said
my husband; and the man gave him two
dollars, and said he considered that a very
large price—more than he could earn in a
whole day. The next happy man was
more liberal: he gave two dollars and
twenty-five cents. But this was quite as
good pay as that received by our friend
the Rev. Mr. H——, of a neighboring
town, who went several miles into the country to marry a couple; after the ceremony
the man said he had no money, but had
some very nice pups, which were as good
as money, and the minister could have one
of them.

When Thanksgiving Day came we received a very pleasant surprise. A young
lady kindly offered to care for the children
in the evening and let me go to church.
We were very much disappointed to find
absent so many whom we expected to see
there, and after service those who were

present hastened from the house, scarcely stopping to speak to us. We went slowly home, thinking it very strange that our friends should act in such a manner. But when we opened the door, there stood a table loaded with a bountiful supper, and the rooms were full of smiling faces. All that before seemed strange was now accounted for, and our hearts were gladdened with such a token of the love and esteem of those with whom we were laboring for the Master.

We were fortunate enough this autumn to get our house plastered; it was the first plastered house in the town.

During the winter my husband was called to visit a dying man who lived in a little cabin about seven miles from the town. The sick man was about sixty years of age, and had a wife, a daughter and two sons living with him. He had been ill with malarial fever, which soon threw him into quick consumption. He was now dying,

9

but not without the strong abiding faith in the Lord Jesus that always casts a shining lustre on the pathway to the tomb. He conversed freely with my husband about his departure to the other world, and just before his spirit left the falling house of clay he opened his dim eyes and, gazing upward, cried out, "Oh, that beautiful river!" A young man noted for his profanity was standing by the bedside watching the change that came gradually over the features of this aged veteran of the cross. As a neighbor closed the eyes of the good old man the young man said to him, "Mr. S——, I never realized it before; but it is an awful thing to die." From that time he began to give his heart to the Lord and call upon the name of Christ, whose " blood cleanseth from all sin," that he might "die the death of the righteous, and that his last end might be like his." So far as I know, he never uttered another oath.

This young man had been deeply and truly in love with the daughter of the man who had now departed this life, and had sought her heart and hand, but was persistently refused on account of his profanity and wickedness. The father of the young lady had not long been laid away when she was taken with a cough, and in a short time the physician said he could do nothing for her; she had pulmonary consumption. She had become so changed and emaciated that all knew she would follow her father in a few months. The young man had now given up his evil habits and was living a life of prayer, but he still loved her, and again asked her to be his wife. She said she could live only a short time, and such a union would make parting more bitter. The young man insisted upon marrying her and taking her to his home to care for her while she did live. In a few days they came to our house and were united in marriage. I thought it was one of the most solemn scenes I had ever witnessed —a trembling, wasted form leaning against a strong young man, vowing to be his faith· ful, loving wife until death. The slender, delicate hand that was clasped in his was not that of a beautiful bride who expected a life of happiness in this world, but one that soon must be given up to the icy grasp of Death ; the crimson glow upon her cheek was not the healthful flush that adorns the features of the happy young bride, but simply the sign-painting of Death, where in fever-letters I could read the solemn words, " Be ye also ready." As I looked into her large bright eyes I thought, " Must they so soon be closed upon the one who would gladly give his life for her?" Her lips were parched and quivering, and as the tears dropped from her blue eyes others were rolling down the cheeks of the young man who stood by her side. Her husband took her to his home and watched over her day and night. She was very patient, and daily led her kind companion nearer and nearer the dear Saviour who was now her comfort and support, and who had promised to accompany her through the dark valley of death. But she soon died, in her husband's arms; and, though he wept bitterly over her sleeping form, he has learned to love the Saviour in whom she trusted, and through whose death, merits and intercession he expects to meet the loved one where death has no claim.

My husband again endeavored to hold a protracted meeting, but the wicked and profane resolved to break up the services and turn the schoolhouse into a dancing-hall. The board of trustees were ungodly men, and in his sermons he reproved their wickedness; so they determined to put an end to his preaching in the schoolhouse. They accordingly locked the door. On Sunday morning a great many came to the house, and, not being able to enter, went away. Many of the people were so displeased with this act of the trustees that they said they would never again support them for any office. The trustees, finding that they had incurred the disapprobation of the peo- ple, soon unlocked the door and gave their consent to our having religious services in the house. But for a long time they would gather in that house every Saturday night and dance until nearly daylight, and on Sunday mornings the schoolhouse would be in a condition not very befitting a place of worship. The seats would be all thrown out and piled on the ground, the stove put in one corner of the room and the floor covered with dirt.

My husband was advised by some very good people not to preach against dancing, because they thought that by such preach- ing certain ones might be kept away who otherwise would be benefited, and perhaps won, by the glorious gospel of the Son of

God. He concluded to take their advice, but soon learned that dancing men and women were not apt to be won by the gospel unless the Spirit of God first made them sick of sin, and that it was better to obey the injunction of Scripture which says, "Reprove, rebuke, exhort with all long-suffering."

CHAPTER XI.

BAD INDIANS.

IN the month of March two sisters who had been carried away by the Indians came to our house, and there, from the lips of the eldest, I learned the following sad story:

"We were crossing the plains with an ox-team, going to the Rocky Mountains, and were about fourteen miles from any settlement. We left camp in the morning, and had gone about one hundred yards when seventeen Indians and two squaws came over a little hill from the river. I was about fifty yards from the wagon, with my mother and sister aged fifteen. Four came toward us, and one shot an arrow at me, but it did not hit me. I then ran toward my brother, nineteen years old, who was hunting an antelope. My sister was walking near the wagon with father; my oldest sister was driving the oxen. We had two cows and two yearlings tied behind the wagon. The Indians shot my father through the back; he fell, and never moved. My oldest sister jumped out of the wagon with the axe, and ran to them and struck one on the arm and knocked the gun out of his hands, but another shot her dead. Mother ran to father and knelt down over him, and they shot her; she fell by his side. As I ran toward my brother I saw him fall: an Indian called Medicine Water shot him. I ran back to the wagon. The Indians stood me by the side of my sister fifteen years old, and after they had looked at us a moment they shot my sister. They scalped my mother and oldest sister, both of whom had long hair. I was in hopes they would kill us all. One was about to shoot my little sister of five, but one of the squaws took her from before the gun and saved her life. My other sister, of seven, they decided to take with them. The squaw who saved my little sister took her on her pony, and an Indian tied the one of seven to his saddle behind him. They put me on one pony, and my other living sister on another. In a short time they tore all our clothing from us and gave us an old blanket each, and in this condition we traveled nearly two weeks. We had something to eat once a day nearly all the time, but sometimes only every other day.

"The Indians carried mother's and sister's scalps in front of us, hanging to the points of their spears and bows. They did not wash off the blood, and no one can imagine how we felt.

"After a while the troops came near, and the savages left our little sisters on the prairie, but took us and fled. I was much in hopes the soldiers would find us, but they did not then. After six days some of the Indians went back to that place and found our sisters who had been left, and brought them into the new camp. We were very glad to see them alive. Whilst alone on the prairie they wandered up and down the stream, and found the place where the soldiers had camped and left some crackers and dry bread and scraps of meat, on which they lived; they told us that some dogs came up one night and walked around and smelt them, but we knew it must have been wolves.

"The Indians had a fearful war-dance over the scalps of our mother and sister. After we camped for the winter each of us had the wood to gather for one lodge. The weather was very cold, and I froze my feet so that my toe-nails came off. We were whipped and starved by the squaws. Our only hope was that we should be found by the troops. After untold suffering we were

surrounded by the soldiers, and the Lord
only knows how happy we were to find
ourselves once more with white men."

I have endeavored to give a statement
of the facts of the painful and heartrending endurances of these young girls as
near as I can remember their conversation
with me, and also from a few notes taken
by my husband at the time. But the sad
countenances, the melancholy tones, the
emaciated forms, the watery eyes, the
browned skin and parched lips, told more
plainly the tale of wretchedness and horror than words could possibly do. These
girls were very intelligent, and I should
judge that before their captivity they were
unusually handsome. After they were re-
captured they were taken to the nearest
settlement, where they might receive clothing and have an opportunity to rest and
rally from their prostrate condition. The
lady where they were taken said she never
saw such objects of pity in her life; their

slender limbs, scratched and bruised and bleeding, were but partially covered with the old dingy and greasy blankets which they endeavored to hold around their wasted forms.

I leave my readers to fill up the true picture by imagining themselves in the place of sensitive and delicate girls. Destruction comes upon them while in the midst of the family and under the care and smiles of loving parents, and sweeps them away from all earthly peace and joy. They see their parents fall without the opportunity of saying farewell to their children. They see their brother drop from his horse to suffer and die alone on the plains, with no kind friend to moisten his dying lips. They behold their sisters pierced by Indian bullets, and witness deeds still more atrocious and heartrending. They stand silent and speechless and see the scalps torn from the heads of their mother and sister. They see the bodies mutilated in a shock-

ing manner, then covered with their bedding, dry grass and portions of their
wagon, and burned. All this takes place
in a few moments, and the unfortunate
captives find themselves tied on Indian
ponies and moving rapidly over the plains,
every leap of the ponies carrying them
farther and farther from the smouldering
remains of their parents and sisters and
all white settlements. The Indians have no
mercy upon them, and during the long day
they are jolted and jostled along through
the dry grass by the plunging ponies.
They know it is not a dream, a horrible
nightmare, for they see the dark hair of
their mother and their sister waving before
them in the breeze. They come to a stream,
and the ponies stop to drink; and here the
poor sufferers look down in the clear water
and wish they might be buried there for
ever, but they are bound to the beasts that
are carrying them. In a zigzag path they
ascend the other bank, and are soon put-

ting distance between them and the leafless branches of the trees. Finally night
comes down upon them, and they know
not where they are. The Indians are happy, seeming to rejoice over the misery of
their captives. A blazing fire is made,
which shines through the tree-tops, but
it does not cheer the throbbing hearts of
the sorrow-stricken girls. Near the fire
are driven in the ground, two stakes on
which are hung the flowing tresses of their
sister and the locks of their mother, which
are slightly intermingled with gray. They
had looked upon those locks from their
earliest recollections, their little hands had
dallied with them in their infancy, but they
never expected to see that loved hair a tro-
phy of savages—the object of a frightful Indian war-dance away on the plains. Around
these scalps their captors and tormentors
commence their orgies, and as they whirl
around and leap the night is made dismal
with their unearthly yells, which drown the

faint moans and sighs of the defenceless
girls, who lean their weary heads upon
each other.   They cannot eat, but, weary
and exhausted, they soon fall asleep ; yet
in their dreams they see the bloody knife,
and dying groans disturb their slumbers.
In the morning the sun shines brightly
upon them, but how differently are they
situated from what they were the morning before, when all was prosperous and
joyous around them !

This is no exaggerated picture of the
imagination ; indeed, it fails to present to
the mind of the reader half the depths of
misery into which these girls, and many
others like them, have been plunged by
these cruel murderers of the plains.
Those who live on the extreme frontier,
and thus prepare the way for permanent
settlement and good society, live in constant dread of the outrages of the Indians ;
and not without cause.

I have seen our little town full of them,

their red blankets flashing in every direction. They would purchase tobacco, coffee, sugar, bacon, fowls and fruit, and, in fact, everything they desired, and with plenty of money they would prowl around through the country, following the different streams, to the great terror of women and children : and often they would commit the most foul and bloody deeds, the blame of which not unfrequently they endeavored to charge on other tribes.

A number of men had been killed and scalped in the cedar hills. The settlers along the stream resolved to prepare for an attack, which they expected every day. A party was soon detected coming toward the settlement. A number of young men mounted their horses and rode out to meet them, and made signs for them to go back. They paid no attention, but continued to approach, carrying their rifles in front of them. The settlers fired the first volley, killing two or three, and the others fled.

10

In a few days I read an account of this in an Eastern paper, which said a party of civil Indians passing through a settlement, hunting buffalo, were attacked by the settlers and several of them killed. This I knew to be a serious mistake. Why did they come into the white settlement to hunt buffalo?

Two of another tribe went to a cabin where a woman was alone with her two children, her husband being absent. They asked the woman for bread and meat and coffee; she brought forward the food and placed it on the table, but the bread was corn-bread. The Indians looked at the woman and said, with a scowl, "Biscuit!" She said she had no flour in the house, and could make them no biscuit. One of the Indians said, "White woman lie!" The woman then took her husband's revolver from a shelf, leveled it at his head and said, "Now you go!" They left the house, begging her, "Not shoot! Good Indian!"

Some of the Indians came to a party of surveyors near our town and told them that they had just killed three men, and said, "You can find them covered up in the sand," at such a place. The surveyors went to the spot, and found the dead bodies as the Indians had said. They were young men, and all had been scalped. About the same time one of our neighbors (his name was Watkins) was killed and scalped near his own home, and a party of freighters were tied to their wagons and burned.

Settlers on the frontier who have suffered and seen others suffer thus must be pardoned if they show less love for the Indians than those who live a thousand miles away from them.

Yet many of these cruel and bloodthirsty wild men of the plains have been brought to the Saviour, and are now not only good citizens, but earnest and efficient workers in the cause which we all so much desire to see progressing.

CHAPTER XII.

THE INFIDEL.

DURING the winter my husband went to W—— to hold a protracted meeting. While stopping at the hotel a gentleman said, "Here is Mr. B——, one of the best men in town, but he is killing himself with strong drink. Go and see him; if your religion can do any good for him, I will have some confidence in it."

"Where is he?" said my husband.

"You will find him around one of the saloons," was the reply.

My husband then went to one of the saloons and asked if Mr. B—— was there. They pointed to a sad, forlorn-looking fellow and said that was Mr. B——. He told him that he would like to go with him to his room, as he wanted to talk with him a few moments. "All right," replied Mr. B——, and then accompanied my husband to his room, which was a miserable one over a handsome store.

My husband conversed with him, asking him many questions. He learned that Mr. B—— was from Vermont; that his mother was living and an earnest Christian woman, ever praying for him; that he knew he was killing himself drinking whisky; that he was unhappy and miserable and wanted to reform. Then my husband asked him if he had ever thought of what Jesus had said: "Come unto me, all ye that labor and are heavy laden, and I will give you rest." Here Mr. B—— burst into loud sobs and tears; so that his cries were heard in the street below. My husband then asked him if he would kneel down while he prayed for him. He said, "Yes, I will," falling on his knees at the same moment.

After spending a short time in prayer they arose, and Mr. B—— continued to wipe the tears from his eyes with his old sleeve, at the same time saying, "God have mercy on my soul!"

That night my husband preached between the two saloons, and the room, which would accommodate about one hundred and fifty persons, was crowded. Mr. B—— while listening outside fell on the sidewalk as though he had been shot, and was immediately carried into one of the nearest rooms. The next day my husband could not see him, as the doctor had forbidden any one except a nurse to talk with him, or even to enter his room.

About a year from this time, while my husband was passing through the town in the stage, he asked the driver how Mr. B—— was prospering. "Nicely," was the reply. "He has not tasted a drop of whisky since the revival last winter; he has two pair of horses, and is now doing well."

My husband also went to E——, forty-five miles from our town, and preached every night for nearly two weeks. Several persons were converted and much good was done; but in the place there was one very wicked infidel who had broken up several meetings and a short time before this had driven a minister out of the town. Several of the citizens warned my husband to be on his guard, for, as some souls were being converted, the devil would not allow this infidel to be quiet.

My husband preached on Sunday morning, and Sabbath-school immediately followed. At the close of the Sabbath-school, before the people had left the schoolhouse, the unbeliever reached him a New Testament with his finger on the twenty-sixth verse of the fourteenth chapter of Luke, and said, with a sneer, "I want you to tell me if you would advise me to leave and hate my wife and children and go after

Jesus Christ. I want you to come and see my wife and little children, and then tell me if you think I ought to hate them and love Christ."

My husband told him he did not understand the Scriptures. He then talked loudly and boisterously, vehemently shaking his fist, and for some time would not give my husband a chance to say a word.

Finally my husband said he would like to ask a few questions. The infidel said, "All right; go ahead." He then asked him if he had been brought up by religious parents.

"I was," he replied.

"Is your mother living?"

"No; she has been dead some time."

"Do you think she was a Christian?"

"Yes, if ever there was one in this world."

"Did she ever pray for you?"

"Yes, many a time;" and here the infidel wiped a tear from his eye. At the same moment he reached my husband one dollar, saying, "Take this and buy a bottle of vinegar bitters ; it is the best ague medicine in the world." My husband took the money and thanked him, and the crowd dispersed, many of the young people laughing heartily.

The next morning he went to the infidel's house. The man's wife seemed like an excellent woman and he had a family of fine children, but the unbeliever would not be persuaded to surrender his heart to the Saviour. The next time my husband was at E—— he was told that the infidel had left his wife and children—not to go with Christ, but with his hired girl.

CHAPTER XIII.

GOD'S DISCIPLINE.

OUR little church at C—— was all this time gradually increasing in numbers, interest and usefulness. But in such a border village, where the only church is composed of members from nearly every Christian denomination, the pastor, and also his wife, must always remember the words of our Lord: "Be ye wise as serpents and harmless as doves."

One of our elders was a good man, but, being influenced by his wife, stayed away from our services and would have nothing to do with the interests of the church. The cause of this offence was my husband's preaching against dancing. This elder and his wife believed it no harm

154

to dance, and consequently encouraged their children in attending the nightly revels, which were conducted in such a manner that it was neither proper nor safe for any respectable lady to attend them. After the whole family had abandoned the church and rented one of their houses for a drinking-saloon, where the poison was daily dealt out to the weak-minded young men of the place, my husband asked two brother-ministers what they thought he ought to do in such a case. They both advised him to have them brought before the session and dealt with according to the rules of the Church. But a complete session could not be had without the head of this family. He finally mentioned the trouble to Rev. Mr. H—— of W——, who advised my husband to use all forbearance and patience. For, said he, "Such a case of discipline would be likely to rend the little church in a sad and lamentable manner." He concluded to take this advice, and presented the whole matter to God, asking him to take the case into his own hands, to chastise the wrong-doers for their waywardness, and to bring them back penitent to the fold.

In a few weeks my husband said he trembled to think in what a fearful way his prayers had been answered. One of the little girls of this family, about eight years of age, was suddenly taken sick, and died. The parents sent for my husband to conduct the funeral service. He addressed them sympathetically and admonished them to let their affections follow the spirit of their dear child to the better world; but after the funeral they remained indifferent to the welfare of the little band of believers who were struggling to hold up the standard of purity and godliness in the dark land of the buffalo and the savage.

In a short time the oldest son was killed in a manner sufficient to try the faith of any parent. The boy was about seventeen years of age a member of the church and naturally a good, quiet boy, but, being allowed by his parents to spend his evenings around the drinking-saloons and to attend the low and boisterous dances, with the excuse that children must have some resort for amusement, he soon concluded that in order to be a man he must, like other young men of the place, carry a revolver. He accordingly purchased one and took it to the saloon. He had been there but a short time before he fell into a dispute with a border ruffian. In order to show his bravery and intimidate his opponent, he raised his revolver with a sort of flourish, but was instantly shot through the head by the other.

The boy had no idea of shooting, for there was no load in his revolver, but he had never learned the fact that on the border a man must never say "shoot" while disputing with another, unless he is an expert in using the weapon and intends to shoot, and that quickly. He did not know that a revolver was a thousand times more of an enemy than a friend to an inexperienced youth like himself.

This was a terrible blow to the parents, but still their hearts were not subdued.

After this the elder daughter was seized with a violent cough. She traveled several hundred miles, and consulted different physicians, but with no good effect; it soon became evident that she must die. After she gave up the last hope of recovering, and her parents knew she would soon leave them, they sent for my husband. As he entered the room where the young woman lay he knew that death was calling. Her long yellow hair, which at one time barely escaped falling into the hands of the Indians, lay in golden waves on the pillow, but, instead of the health-tinted cheeks that she had so often carried to the dancing-room, there was now the pallor of death. She grasped my husband by the hand and through a flood of tears looked him in the face, but said not a word.

In a moment the mother said, "You must forgive my daughter." He said he had nothing to forgive, but she must look to God for pardon in the name of his well-beloved Son, whose blood "cleanseth from all sin."

After the minister had read the Bible and prayed with the dying girl and the sorrowing parents and brothers and sister, the departing one faintly uttered words like these:

"Oh, when I had health and strength, how little did I think of this! If I had my life to live again, how differently would I spend the precious moments! But now I must die. God have mercy—have mercy—mercy! Save my soul!"

As the dying girl said these words the

tears were falling like raindrops from the
eyes of her father.

When my husband came home, I hastened to the house. That night the poor penitent peacefully passed away to join the
blood-washed company in the presence
of "the sinner's Friend." Her young
friends came in, not to greet her within
the merry walls of mirth, but to bid a
long and last adieu to her who had so
often added ringing music to the fleeting
pleasures of the dance.

> " Old Time will fling his clouds ere long
> 　　Upon those sunny eyes ;
> The voice whose every word is song
> 　　Will set itself to sighs ;
> Your quiet slumbers, hopes and fears
> 　　Will chase their rest away ;
> To-morrow you'll be shedding tears :
> 　　Laugh on, laugh on, to-day."

The next Wednesday evening this Scotchman and his wife were at the prayer-meeting, and for the first time for over a year

we heard his voice in prayer. It is blessed for the Christian to know that God
deals with him as a loving father, and not
as an angry judge. Some men's sins go
to judgment before them, and some follow after. Blessed are all whose sins go
over before them, for in the day of reck-
oning they will not be called to account
for them.

Some time before this the Rev. Mr. Wilson came to this region, and was located
twenty-five miles from our town. He built
a little house on a claim in another county,
intending to send for his family. But it was
soon completely demolished by one of the
terrific storms which are so common on the
plains. The boards of which it was built
were scattered in such a manner that many
of them were never found.

After he had been some time at our
county-seat preaching the gospel of Jesus
he said to one of the leading members of
the church, "You business men are all

11

down in the old farm-wagon and invoked the divine blessing. His prayer was humble, personal and earnest. He prayed for his loved ones far away, and my husband, my children and myself were not forgotten. Until late in the night he continued to tell my husband about God's dealings with him and how his prayers had that day been answered. He had been praying for God to provide some means for him to go with his baggage to the nearest railroad-station —a distance of thirty-five miles. He said that during the day his heavenly Father whispered gently to his soul, and said, " My son, don't fret and worry; I will take care of you." And now he felt very thankful and happy, and realized that the arms of Jesus' love were around him.

W—— and O—— were fields that were all white and ready to harvest. Mr. Wilson, though somewhat advanced in years, possessed as much vitality as a young man. He traveled on foot from one town to the other, a distance of twelve miles, and it seemed too bad for such a man to be compelled to leave such a field for the want of an adequate support at the hands of the church. A gentleman at O—— said that when he heard Mr. Wilson preach he always had something to carry away with him.

I know I am safe in saying—and no person of experience will say otherwise—that a minister with a family can live better on a salary of two hundred and fifty dollars a year in an Eastern town than he can on one of five hundred a year on the Western border.

The next Saturday my husband, not having a horse at this time, walked to O——, about forty miles, to attend Brother Wilson's appointment. On Monday, while returning, he took the wrong road and went several miles out of his way. By doing this he came to a settlement late in the afternoon, and stopped at the first cabin and asked if he could get some dinner. The woman of the house went out into the field and gathered a few ears of worm-eaten sod-corn. This she grated and made a little bread, of which, with the addition of some venison, he made a good dinner, and paid her fifty cents. He learned that there were several families living in the settlement, and that there had never been a sermon preached in the place. He thought there was now an opportunity to do good; so he resolved to stay and preach for the people that night. At dark a good congregation gathered in one of the cabins to listen to the glorious old gospel of the Son of God.

The next day he visited the people from house to house, and at night preached in another cabin. The next morning one of the men sent his boy with two ponies to forward him on his journey a distance of five miles. So his losing his way was overruled for good by the God of providence.

CHAPTER XIV.

DEATH IN THE HOME.

IN the following August one of our twin-boys, now nearly four years old, was seized with membranous croup, and after four days of extreme suffering died. When he was first taken, we thought it was only common croup and were not particularly alarmed. On Thursday a gentleman came to the house and told my husband that the next Sunday he was to be married, and asked him if he could perform the cere-mony. He replied that, as he had no ap-pointment at that hour, he could do so. But he did not know that God had made an appointment for him to attend at that hour which would be one of the saddest he ever attended in his life. It was on

Saturday that our boy died. It was the first time death had broken our little band in the land of strangers, and it was so sudden that we were stunned by the terrible blow. We could only whisper, "Thy will, O God, be done!"

We sent to W—— for a minister. Although we had been so long in that region, still the nearest clergyman was twenty-five miles away. He reached our house about the hour at which my husband had agreed to perform the marriage ceremony. He was also a missionary of our Church, and had been at W—— only a few months. He preached a very comforting sermon, and I shall never forget his words to me as we left the house to go to the grave: "Do not grieve about your child: we are short-lived creatures at best."

As we rode toward the graveyard I said to my husband (and oh the bitter anguish of the thought!), "This is the last ride we shall all take together."

In a short time from this we had a visit from the Rev. Mr. Harsen and wife, whose place of residence and missionary field were sixty miles from C———. I can assure my readers that a visit from such Christian friends, at so sad a time and in a place like this, was very comforting.

The first time my husband met this good man was at C———, about one year before we moved there. He preached in the morning the first sermon that was ever heard in that town. His subject was " the penitent thief," a fitting one for such a place. My husband preached in the afternoon. Mr. Harsen at this time was sixty miles from home, looking after the scattered lambs of the fold. One very cold day that same winter my husband was hauling lumber. Mr. Harsen saw him, and, pulling off his overcoat, reached it to him, saying, " Put this on; I see you need it." That night my husband slept on the ground; the wind blew cold from the north, bringing sleet, and then snow; and, had it not been for that coat, he would have suffered very much.

At another time this same servant of God went on horseback to a poor settlement on Sunday afternoon to preach Christ and also to break the bread of life to a little company of believers who had no pastor. As he was returning the sun went down and the heavens were covered with heavy black clouds. When he was about six miles from his home he lost his way, and was soon wandering around in the tall grass, feeling his way through the intense darkness of the night. At this time his congregation were waiting patiently for their minister; but, as he did not come, they became very anxious and desirous of knowing why he was thus detained. Could the wolves have devoured him, or was he lost? Yes, he was actually lost. About the middle of the night he came to an old cabin where no one lived, and after tying his horse to a sunflower-stalk he found a shelter until morning.

In his town or vicinity there were few, if any, poor and sorrowing ones who were not comforted by the presence, counsel and prayers of this devoted servant of Jesus. At one time he invited my husband to go with him to make a few calls. The first house they entered was a little hovel. The man of the house was very low with consumption, and his wife made a living by washing. Mr. Harsen conversed kindly and freely with the sick man, then knelt down by his side and besought the mercy of Jehovah to rest upon him and to bless him and his family, and just before leaving he put some money in the hand of the poor heartbroken woman.

Although this devoted servant of Christ is now laboring for the Master in the East, there are in the West thousands who will remember him with love and gratitude as long as they live. A thousand just such

earnest, self-sacrificing ministers are needed to-day in the great West.

During his visit at the time of our affliction he preached for my husband three
times, and visited a good many of those
with whom he was acquainted. Many of
the rough and ungodly old frontiersmen
were glad to see him, because they respected him as a true and sincere servant
of the most high God.

His wife was an excellent singer, and
one of those sweet and pleasant women
who are so fitted to drive gloom and sadness from the hearts of all with whom they
associate. When they left our home, we
watched their buggy until it disappeared
over the hill, nearly a mile away. Then
we asked God to go with them and to bless
them abundantly.

About two weeks from this time my
youngest child—a little girl whom I had
named Laura, after my dear departed
prairie-sister—was suddenly taken with

the same disease. On the Sabbath-day I had been several miles from home on horseback to assist the parents of a child who had just died; they also had another child very sick. When I returned at night my little darling came running to meet me, and seemed so full of life that I did not dream she was so soon to be taken from me. Being very weary, I retired early. After my husband came home from church he said he feared she was taking the croup, for she had a fever and was covered with an unnatural perspiration. His words startled me as though the house had been shaken by an earthquake. We sent for some of our neighbors and endeavored to check the formation of the false membrane, but all in vain.

In the morning my husband went to W—— in the stage for a physician, but at night he returned alone. The physician arrived the next day. He looked at her and shook his head, saying, "She has lost her voice." I said, "Oh, doctor, can you do nothing for my child? Must she die?" He said, "There is only one hope, and that is very slight: a few such cases have been saved by the surgical operation of tracheotomy, and I will try it if you think best." We told him, if that was the only hope, to do the best he could. In a few moments he was ready. Several of the neighbors were in the room. My husband and I went into another room and fell on our knees. In a short time the doctor tapped on the door and said, "It is all over." I sprang to my feet, ran to the door, and as I opened it I said, "Is she alive?" He said, "No, she is gone." I went into the room to embrace the lifeless form of my dear child, who two days before seemed so full of life. We knew it was God's will and we endeavored to be reconciled, but we feel the aching void until the present time. The physician, who was an upright Christian man, then read a portion of the Holy Scriptures and prayed God to give us strength to endure the sad bereavement.

We could have no sermon preached over our precious babe, as Mr. M—— had left W—— and we knew of no minister nearer than thirty-five miles. But one of our elders prayed at the house, and also at the grave, where we laid her down on her second birthday, by the side of her little brother, and both were buried close to the grave of our dear friend " Duck," whose arms had so often clasped the little ones to as pure a heart as ever beat within a woman's breast. It seemed to me that she would still love and protect my darling babes; and would they not need it in such a cemetery as this, with graves of murderers and thieves on every side?

But was not this viewing this serious subject from a wrong standpoint? Were not the souls of my precious children in the world of glory, near and dear to the spirit of my friend who died in my arms?

But one blow after another had fallen upon me, until, like Job's friends, I felt like sitting down on the ground seven days in silence. The sweetest earthly music had died away in the darkness of the tomb. Two of the bright flowers on the family tree had been smitten by the frost of death. It was autumn to my poor trembling, shivering soul, and the cold drops were raining on the leaves already fallen.

After this two others of our children were very sick, and for a long while we watched them day and night; but finally, with God's blessing, they both recovered. Our faithful friend, the doctor, would accept of no compensation for his unwearied services.

Shortly after this a bill of ten dollars for poor little Laura's coffin was handed in, and we had no money to pay it. Other small bills were pressing heavily upon us, and for a great many days we carried this financial burden; it seemed as though we could not dispose of it. Finally my husband resolved to write to a lady in Ohio who had written us several very encouraging letters, and who had, in connection with the other ladies of the church to which she belonged, sent us much aid after the grasshopper scourge, and tell her how we were situated. In a few days we received forty dollars, which helped us greatly in our straitened and embarrassing circumstances.

We were now receiving only three hundred dollars per year from the Board of Home Missions. The reduction was made on account of the many calls and the scarcity of funds. At such a distance from the railroad all necessaries—groceries especially—were sold at an enormous price.

About this time a young minister was sent to W——, but remained only three months. He told my husband he did not think it was his duty to remain there and ruin his health. He was a fine sermonizer, but had not much of a missionary's spirit.

Our town and neighborhood seemed now to be changing very rapidly for the better. It is true the rough border element continued with us, but now mingled with it were the better principles of the gospel of Christ. We had scattered religious literature for miles in every direction ; one could scarcely enter a cabin without finding tracts from our Board of Publication. People seemed to be thirsting for the bread of eternal life. Quite frequently about this time they would come a distance of ten miles to hear the word of God.

Three Quaker brethren were passing through our town on their way to an Indian agency, but stopped over the Sabbath. My husband, having an appointment to preach in a new school-house four miles east, asked the Quaker brothers if they would go and conduct the service. They said they would, and my husband went five miles in another direction and organized a Sabbath-school. The Quakers went early

12

to the house, and, as they saw no one moving and only a few little cabins in the distance, they thought they might as well go
back, for there would be no one there that
day to preach to. But in a few moments
wagons were seen coming from every direction, and in a short time the house was
crowded.

CHAPTER XV.

A BLESSED HARVEST.

ABOUT the first of the next November my husband again commenced a series of services and preached every night, holding meetings of inquiry after the sermons. During the first week there seemed to be but slight interest manifested, but the little band of Christians began to pray with more earnestness. The prayer of a few Christians, both by day and by night, was, "O Lord, revive thy work! Convict these Christless souls, and may we hear them crying to thee for mercy!"

One night the schoolhouse was crowded, and after my husband had preached from the text, "We beseech you in Christ's stead be ye reconciled to God," a number arose

for prayers, and some said they had decided to come over to the Lord's side.
Strong men wept in every part of the
house. Several little children arose and
said they wanted to love Jesus and go to
heaven. While some one was speaking
a lady began to cry and scream in such
a manner that some thought she was dying
or going into a fit. I went to her and said,
" Mrs. B——, do not allow yourself to be
so excited; please do be quiet," and other
ladies endeavored to pacify her; but, like
blind Bartimeus, she cried the louder for
Jesus to have mercy on her soul and pardon her sins. She sprang to her feet; her
hat fell from her head ; her hair dropped
down over her shoulders and the large
tears rolled over her cheeks. A profane
skeptic said either God Almighty or the
devil was there, he did not know which.
But in a few minutes she became calm,
took her seat, and after looking over the
congregation a moment she began to sing

"Whiter than Snow." On her countenance there was a heavenly smile such as
never beamed there before. She was a
fine singer, but I am sure she had never
sung as she sang that night. There was
not a dry eye in the house, and many
sobbed aloud. About a dozen young
ladies who previous to this had cared
but little for anything else than to romp
and dance now kneeled down and asked
God to wash them in Jesus' blood and
make them "whiter than snow." By this
time crowds were gathered around every
window. The service continued until nearly midnight.

This glorious work went on until the
place seemed completely revolutionized.
The saloons were comparatively deserted ;
quietness and decorum existed throughout
the town and country—not only on the
Sabbath, but also during the week. Twenty converts united with our little church, and
two other churches received a good many

members.   One church had been organized
previous to the revival, and the other after,
but, as the inhabitants of the place consisted largely of a floating population, many
who received the blessing and participated
in the revival did not unite with any church,
as they expected soon to leave the town.
Thus the spirit and the power of the gospel were carried in burning hearts to other
places, and the great day alone will reveal
the amount of good accomplished during
this glorious refreshing from on high.

When so many of the young men and
women of the place came forward to receive the ordinance of baptism and unite
with the church on profession of their faith,
we indeed saw the silver lining to the black
and heavy clouds which had been hanging
so heavily over us for these many years.
It had been a long, dark night, but the rosy
light of the morning could now be seen;
and it was with great joy that we could
exclaim, "'The winter is past, the rain is

over and gone; the flowers appear on the
earth; the time of the singing of birds is
come, and the voice of the turtle is heard
in our land.' 'They that sow in tears shall
reap in joy. He that goeth forth and weep-
eth, bearing precious seed, shall doubtless
come again with rejoicing, bringing his
sheaves with him.'"

After the revival the people made us a
very surprising donation. Although the
night chosen by our friends was cold and
disagreeable, they came from miles around
and filled our little house, and spread a
bountiful table with more luxuries than
we had seen since coming from the East—
roast chicken, cakes, pies and fruit in abun-
dance; and when the company dispersed,
they left us not only many valuable articles
of provision, but also about forty dollars
in money. One man, who was not a
church-member, said, "Mr. Rideout has
preached and labored among us all these
years, and we have paid him but a mere

trifle.   He has been willing to rough it and live as the rest of us have lived, and certainly we should begin to pay him for his services."

The people were now greatly encouraged; the prospects for a railroad to the town were good, and we all believed that our town and neighborhood had seen their darkest days.

CHAPTER XVI.

SHADOW AND SUNSHINE.

AS the soft south wind began to blow over the prairie, bringing with it gentle showers, and the daisies and the violets were seen in sheltered places along the streams, and the branches of the trees were so loaded with blackbirds I could almost imagine them as being burdened with animated fruit, and the clear water of Fall Creek was splashing musically over the rocks, forming the falls from which it derived its name, there was only gloom and sadness locked in my own heart. I say "locked" because I never told my grief to others. While I knew that "earth has no sorrow that heaven cannot heal," I also knew that earth has sorrows that heaven does not heal in this life.

185

When Jesus said to his disciples, "In the world ye shall have tribulation," I believe he meant until the end of this life; and, while there are thousands of happy and rejoicing Christians in our world, I believe our heavenly Father has, and until the end of time will continue to have, his suffering witnesses. When our Saviour was on earth, he had not even a place to rest his weary head: "Jesus a man of constant grief, a mourner all his days." And many of the blood-washed company who are now praising God among "the spirits of the just made perfect" passed all the way through this world in the bloodstained footsteps of their blessed Master:

"Once they were mourners here below,
And wet their couch with tears."

One bright day my little boy, whose mate had died, came in and said, "Mamma, where is Percy? Why don't he come home?"

I told him Percy was in heaven. He

then looked up with tears in his eyes and said,

"Will he never come back to play with me any more?"

I replied,

"No; you will never see your little brother again in this world."

He then said,

"I want him to come home, so I can give him some of my pretty flowers."

After this, for months, as I would see my dear lonely little boy at play, the words of Mrs. Hemans kept ringing constantly through my mind:

> "Go, call my brother back to me:
> I cannot play alone.
> The spring returns with flower and bee:
> Where has my brother gone?"

This spring I often scattered tears over the little grave on the lonely prairie. How sweet were the flowers that bloomed over the lowly bed of my sleeping children! How richly did the setting sun shine upon

the high waves of the rolling prairie!
What beautiful birds did I see around
those graves! How lightly did the tender blades of grass bow before the breeze!
Yet what deathly silence reigned there! I
scarcely dared to speak aloud; tears flowed
without a sigh or a groan. Even my
prayers were smothered to a whisper.
None but the loving mother who has
laid her little ones away under like circumstances can understand my grief. But
in the midst of all this sorrow there was
one joyful thought: "There is sweet rest
in heaven." This thought was particularly precious, on account of the fact that for
more than five years I had been surrounded by those whose daily cry seemed
to be,

"O land of rest, for thee I sigh!
    When will the moment come
When I shall lay my armor by
    And dwell with Christ at home?"

On every flower that looked sweetly to-

ward the sun, on every leaf that fluttered
in the breeze and on every sunbeam that
smiled through our window-pane seemed
to be written the precious word "Rest."
I heard it in every murmur of the wind
and in every warble of the lark. I saw
it on the pale features of my friends as
one after the other their weary heads
were laid on their coffin-pillow. There
were a few wealthy ones in the vicinity,
but on every side were poverty, sickness
and death.

One day my husband was called to go to
an adjoining county to attend the funeral
of a young man who had died with pneu-
monia, and his little nephew, who died
about the same time. This family were
the only white people who lived in the
county. A great many went from C——
to the one sad and gloomy home in H——
County. My husband said it was a scene
he could never forget. The dug-out was
long and narrow and the day was cloudy

and dark. In the end farthest from the
door, in one corner, lay the body of the
young man whose spirit had returned "to
God who gave it," and directly opposite,
in the other corner, lay his brother—another young man—very low with the same disease. My husband endeavored to talk with
him about his spiritual condition and his
prospects of "glory, honor and immortality
beyond the grave," but it was so dark that
the face of the young man could scarcely
be seen. My husband, by stooping very
low, could barely detect the feeble motion
of his lips and the occasional lifting of his
eyelids, but could not understand a word
he endeavored to utter. He then prayed
for the Lord to raise him up; and in due
time God answered his prayer, for the
young man was restored to health.

The father of the young men stood weeping in the centre of the dug-out, and *his*
father—an old man of more than eighty
years—leaned his wrinkled forehead against

the wall, of " Mother Earth." There were present several women who lived in our county, but near this dug-out. How pale and wretched they looked! Fever and ague seemed to be written upon the pallid cheeks, the bloodless lips and the sunken eyes. On a dry knoll near the dug-out they lowered the young man into his grave, and his little nephew by his side, the first known grave of a white man in this county.

" Howl, O ye winds, around this grave,
    And, grasses, burn, and, coyotes, bark!
  Ye cannot wake the sleeping ones
    Till Christ shall bid them rise, depart!"

Yet with these dark shadows all was not gloom, and we turned from them to fields on which the bright sunshine gleamed.

This summer our Sabbath-school was in a flourishing condition; nearly every one seemed to be interested in having it prosper. On the Fourth of July we had a nice picnic for the school. The merchants gave candy, raisins, nuts, etc., to make the little ones happy. The children formed a procession at the schoolhouse and marched to a lovely grove by the side of a sparkling little stream, carrying a banner on which was inscribed "Stand up for Jesus." Seats had been previously arranged, and a large company gathered in the grove and the day passed pleasantly to all. It was a great pleasure to us to see so many taking such an interest in the Sabbath-school.

During the five years my little class had increased from two—and they my own children—to more than twenty, all happy little boys and girls except one, and she an Indian girl nearly grown, but as childish as any in the class. A lady in the town gave her a night-dress trimmed a little with embroidery; the next Sabbath she wore it to school as an outer dress, tied around the waist with a pink ribbon. She always paid good attention, and was greatly pleased with the little papers and cards given her.

We could only account for the fact that nearly all the people of the place seemed to be interested in the church and Sabbath-school by believing that it was the work of God in fulfillment of his promise that his word should not return unto him void, but that it should accomplish that whereunto he sent it.

One Sunday morning about three years before this time my husband left our " Family Bible " in the schoolhouse, intending to preach again in the evening, but during the day some rough and ungodly fellows went in and tore the Bible in pieces, scattering the leaves from one side of the house to the other and trampling them beneath their feet. Near the door, and nearly covered with mud, lay the covers, still bearing the inscription " Holy Bible," but by ungodly hands they had been robbed of their precious contents. That Bible we had brought with us from the old " Pine Tree State ;" it contained a concordance and a dictionary,

also essays on the authenticity of the Scriptures and Doddridge's sermons on the evi-
dences of Christianity and our Family Rec-
ord.   We considered it a serious loss.
But the devil could not destroy the work
in this way, for the leaven was already
working in many hearts, and with God's
blessing it continued to work until many
precious souls were brought into the king-
dom of our Lord Jesus Christ.

CHAPTER XVII.

FRUITS OF FAITHFULNESS.

THE following summer my labors seemed as arduous as ever. My husband made it a rule to visit all strangers as soon as they moved into the neighborhood and invite them to our services; accordingly, on the Sabbath, people often came six or eight miles to hear the gospel.

One man lived five miles from town, in a little log cabin. He was very poor. He had a yoke of oxen, but one died, and he worked the other alone. My husband was passing the cabin, and resolved to go in and talk with the family about their souls' salvation. This man was considered one of the worst men living in that region; he was known by the name of "Old John."

When my husband went into the cabin the family received him very kindly, and after conversing a while with them he asked if they had a Bible. The woman went to a box, took out an old leather-covered Bible and handed it to him. He read a portion from that blessed book, and then knelt down and prayed for the blessing of God to rest on the family.

In a short time this poor man purchased another ox, and regularly every Sabbath he came with his wife and little girl and several of his neighbors and their children to church and Sabbath-school. The whole family united with the church, and seemed to rejoice that the Lord had sent some one to reclaim them and draw them to the Saviour. They had been members of the Presbyterian Church in other days.

My husband preached in the schoolhouse every Sabbath morning, and we had Sabbath-school in the afternoon, which he did not attend, as he had appointments at dif-

ferent places in the country to preach in
the afternoon, but he came back to town
and preached in the evening. Many who
came to the morning service, wishing to
remain to the evening meeting, would go
home with us ; and thus the day which was
given for rest was often for me the hardest
day of the seven. I generally prepared
dinner for from six to twelve besides my
own family, and, as my husband was the
only minister of any denomination nearer
than twenty-five miles, we had a large
number of callers during the week.

Often poor people coming into the neighborhood without home or money would
come to our house for shelter until
they could build a cabin or dug-out, and
against such our doors were never closed.
During the rainy season those who lived
on the bottom lands were often driven
from their dug-outs by rising streams
flooding the low lands of the country. I
have seen the water flowing through the

tops of large cottonwood trees with the force of a mighty river, and the bottom lands would resemble great lakes. During such times as these many would seek shelter beneath our roof.

Mr. M——, who had recently come from the East, looked at this with surprise, if not with indignation. Visiting us when our house was full, he said that Mrs. M—— would not be imposed upon in such a manner a single moment. I told him to wait until they had been in the West a year, and perhaps they would both think differently.

Some time after this a young man who was more willing to beg than to work called at the house of Brother M—— late in the evening and wanted supper, lodging and breakfast. Mr. M—— said, "We cannot accommodate you; you will have to go to the hotel." But the young man replied that he had no money, and insisted on staying, claiming a right to the minister's hospitality. Brother M—— then took the young man to the hotel and told the land-lord to furnish him supper, bed and break-fast and he would pay the bill. It is no light affair for one who claims to be led by the Spirit of Christ to turn away one who asks for food and shelter.

This summer an aged minister and his wife moved into our town, where they lived a short time, and then they built a sod house. Such a house is made by plough-ing a piece of prairie and then cutting the sod in square pieces and laying it up like bricks in a brick house. This is covered with dirt, leaving the ground for a floor. The old lady hung sheets around the walls, which, after hanging her pictures, gave the cabin a neat, cozy appearance. She said it was much better than no home, but she lived in daily dread of visits from snakes.

A short time before this one of our neighbor's children—their only girl, about three years old—was playing near the door when she was bitten on her foot by a very small rattlesnake. The bite was so trifling that her mother did not apprehend the least danger, and consequently she did nothing for the child for several hours. As the wound, which at first resembled two very slight scratches of a pin, began to assume a more serious aspect, and her foot became seriously swollen and inflamed, they sent for a physician, who told the parents that the child was in a very critical condition. After several months of extreme suffering the little girl began to recover, but it was feared she would be a cripple, as a large portion of the flesh dropped from her foot and ankle. If the mother had been supplied with spirits of ammonia, and had applied it immediately to the wound, how much misery she would have saved her little daughter! How essential it is for parents to watch their children and apply the proper remedies, both physical and moral, before it is too late!

A business man of our village came to my husband and said, "There is a man in the town whom I have decided to kill." He then held up a new revolver, which he said he had purchased for that very purpose. My husband, already knowing something about the cause of this hasty decision on the part of this man, asked him why he had decided to commit such a terrible deed.

The man replied that he had hired Mr. C—— and had been paying him good wages, but that, instead of taking an interest in his business, he had become wonderfully interested in his family.

My husband said, "Does your wife care anything for him?"—"Indeed she does," was the reply; "she loves him dearly, for she told me so this morning." He also said he had forbidden Mr. C—— to speak to his wife, but it did no good, as they improved every opportunity to talk to each other. "And now," he continued, "I am determined to kill him, if I do not live another minute."

My husband said, "You must not do it. You must not make yourself wretched for life. You had better give up your wife, if she cares more for him than she does for you. Think of the many poor fellows who are now wretched and miserable on account of like deeds performed in such haste. If you take the life of this man, your wife will certainly leave you. You will always be followed by rippling streams of blood, and his dying groans will disturb the latest moments of your life. Now, take the advice of a friend, and remember that if you commit such a crime you will repent of it a thousand times."

The man answered that perhaps that was all true, but he would rather die than have his family broken up by such an intruder.

My husband advised him to rule his spirit and not be hasty; to ask God to di-

rect him aright, to converse with his wife
on the subject of her duty to God and to
God's law and call, and to pray with her
and ask her to love Jesus.

He said he would try it. He did so, and
the next Sabbath they both united with the
church; and in less than a week Mr. C——
left the place, and we saw him no more.

> " When Christians pray the devil runs,
>   And leaves the field to Zion's sons."

About this time my husband received a
note from a gentleman who lived six miles
in the country, saying that a member of
his family had become very anxious con-
cerning the future life, and desired him to
come over immediately. When he arrived
at the house the lady told him that her
daughter, about fourteen years of age, was
so distressed on account of her sins that
she could neither eat nor sleep, but continued to cry day and night. Her mother
said that for several weeks her daughter's

grief had become deeper and deeper, and all on account of the belief that she was too great a sinner to be saved. My husband conversed with her a long time, endeavoring to explain the Scriptures and show her that she must put her trust in Christ for the forgiveness of her sins, until she said she began to feel as though she might be saved. After he prayed with them she became quite joyful, and asked her mother if she could join the church. But her mother thought she had better wait a while; she did not think it best for young people to be too hasty. But the girl soon united with the church, and what a faithful little Christian she continued to be!

One place where my husband preached was in a schoolhouse three miles from this girl's home, and every Sabbath on which he held service there she came to hear the gospel which she loved. One Sabbath morning the congregation gathered, but

Emma was not there. My husband won-
dered why she was absent; but about the
time he commenced his sermon he looked
out of the window and saw her coming
through the grass, which in many places
was higher than her head. She was late,
and had left the road to come through the
tall grass in her haste to get there in
time.

By this time the people in the town and
through the country had become much interested in the welfare of the little church
that had been planted under so many difficulties. The tender plant had taken root
in the wild and uncultivated soil of the distant prairie, and, being warmed by the rays
of the Sun of righteousness, it had flour-
ished like the cedars of Lebanon. The
tramp of the buffalo did not injure it; the
terrible prairie fires, with flames darting
thirty feet in the air, could not burn it; the
drouth could not wither it, for it was wa-
tered with tears; the Indian's arrow could

not penetrate it, for it had on the "armor of God;" and after the grasshoppers had devoured every green thing for many miles around, the air was still fragrant with the flowers that bloomed on this heavenly plant. It caused the wilderness and the solitary places to be glad, for in the desert it rejoiced and "blossomed like the rose." The Indian saw it, and the knife dropped from his hand; the thief saw it, and the stolen horse was returned; the murderer saw it, and his weapon was thrown into the stream; and many a weary soul found a resting-place beneath the branches of this gospel tree.

The doctor on whose office floor my husband had slept so many nights deeded twelve lots to the trustees of the church. He did this only a few days before he died, in Quincy, Illinois, and now an effort was made to raise money for the purpose of building an edifice. Five hundred dollars were subscribed, besides town lots and labor, and arrangements were made to build the church the next spring.

In November my husband went to W—— again to hold a series of meetings, but was there only a few days when he had a serious attack of pleurisy. Dr. C—— advised him to give up preaching and go home and rest.

When he returned, I was very busy assisting the ladies in preparing for a festival on Thanksgiving. It was to be the first effort of the kind ever made at C——, and we were much interested in its success, as the proceeds were to be invested in a Christmas tree for the Sabbath-school. It was very cold on the night of the festival, but many more were there than we expected. I was very busy all the evening, and felt quite happy to see so many present.

While there I sought an opportunity to ask our physician—a young man who had been at C—— only a few months—what he thought about the condition of my husband's health. His reply was something like this: "Your husband is a candidate for consumption ; and unless he gives up preaching and stays in the house when the weather is cold or stormy and takes the very best care of himself, he will die in less than a year." This unexpected message disqualified me for any further duties of the evening. In a few moments a lady asked me why I was so nervous and what made my hands tremble. I told her what the doctor had just told me, and to comfort me she said that was the general opinion of the people. I left the room as soon as possible, and, hastening home, told my husband what the doctor had said. He replied : "I shall preach the gospel as long as I can, and leave the result with God." He continued to grow worse, and was not able to preach again until the 1st of January.

On Christmas Eve the schoolhouse was crowded ; there was a present for every child that belonged to the school, and candy and popcorn for every one in the house. The Indian girl of my class was there; she received a silk necktie, but brought it to me and said she did not want it, but she wanted a little doll.

14

CHAPTER XVIII.

THE CLOSE OF THE CONFLICT.

ONE cold day I called on a Mrs. H——. She was a Christian, but her husband had been a degraded inebriate who for several months had been endeavoring to reform. After I had entered the house and seated myself in a chair, this woman came and dropped her head in my lap and wept bitterly. She said her little home was gone and they would be turned out of doors with no shelter from the cold storms of winter. After weeping a long time she wiped her eyes with her apron, and, rocking herself to and fro, said, "What shall I do? My health is not good; this is my only dress, and here are my children covered with rags. My little home is gone, my husband is again intoxicated, and I know not which way to turn."

The house in which they lived had belonged to her, and, as her husband had been sober for several weeks, she had sold the house with the intention of building another on a claim two miles from the town. But, instead of going to the railroad herself to purchase the lumber, she sent her husband, who by this time had so greatly improved that she imagined he could never be intoxicated again. But, once within the city, old associates gathered around him, and ere he was aware he had fallen a victim to the monster that "biteth like a serpent and stingeth like an adder." After several days he returned, a poor miserable drunkard, without a foot of lumber or a dollar of his wife's money. After the poor fellow became sober he wept bitterly, and asked God to forgive him and to give him strength to overcome the evil. He soon

united with the church, and I have never
known or heard of his being intoxicated
since.

My husband preached nearly every Sabbath through the remainder of the winter,
but did not attempt to hold a series of
special meetings. A few united with the
church; the congregations were good, and
the Sabbath-school was very interesting and
well attended. But I noticed that his
cough continued, and as the weather began to grow warm he commenced to fail
very fast. I asked the doctor what I could
do for him: he said there was a possibility
that a trip to the Rocky Mountains would
benefit him. I went home and told him we
would go to Colorado. To this he replied
that it would never do for us to go among
strangers with our young family and him--
self an invalid. I told him if I had health
I could make a living for the family in the
mountains, and we would go, trusting the
Lord to care for us.

The 1st of April we bade farewell to our friends and started for the town of E——, where our Presbytery was to meet, nearly a hundred miles from our home. Our conveyance was a common farm-wagon drawn by a pair of very slow mules. One of the elders of the church and his wife accompanied us.

The first day we came to W——. The next day we expected to reach the nearest railroad town; but when we were within twelve miles of that town the sun went down, and it was soon dark. About ten o'clock we missed the road, and found ourselves wandering on the prairie. In crossing a ravine the mules and wagon sank in the mud. After a long time we succeeded in extricating the mules, but the wheels of the wagon were sunk so deep that we could not move them. My husband started on one of the mules to find some one to assist us. The elder and his wife and myself pulled dry grass and kept a blazing fire for a beacon-light for him. After two or three hours he came back, bringing another man, with a team and a spade, and by the light of our grass fire they succeeded in freeing the wagon from the "miry clay." After we were safely out of the "Slough of Despond" we went to the house of the man who assisted us, and remained until morning. It was a log cabin, and we all slept on the floor.

The next day, at ten o'clock, we reached the railroad, and I saw a train of cars for the first time in more than six years. I also heard a church-bell ring; there was music in it, for I had not heard such a sound in all these years.

When we were on our way to N—— we passed through this town, and there were then about one hundred inhabitants. Lots were selling on the main street for twenty-five dollars each. There was no railroad, and the town consisted of a few little cabins away on the prairie. But now all was changed. It was a railroad town of nearly seven thousand inhabitants, with solid blocks of brick houses and capacious churches, and, instead of lots selling for twenty-five dollars, they were worth from one thousand to five thousand dollars.

Here I met several of my friends who had lived at C——, among others Mrs. S——, a woman who seemed to scorn and laugh at everything of a religious nature when we first went to C——; but during a night of the manifestation of God's power to save, although she was dressed in costly garments, she knelt down on the floor of the schoolhouse and there gave her heart to the Saviour. She was now living in this place, and I was happy to find that she was still living in the triumphs of faith. I also met a young girl about fifteen years of age who was converted during the revival at C——. I think she was one of the sweetest little Christians I ever saw; but she said the people there were not very friendly, and she thought it was on account of her clothing not being very nice. I told her to introduce herself to the minister, and he would make her feel at home in the church and Sabbath-school.

The next day we went to E——, a distance of thirty miles, to attend the Presbytery, but I did not enjoy the exercises very much. The ride of one hundred miles over the prairie had exhausted me, and the hotel where we stopped was nearly a mile from the church.

My husband coughing day and night and the sad thought of leaving our friends at C—— and going to a strange land with only one hundred dollars to pay all our expenses,—these things so burdened my mind that I was glad when the Presbytery adjourned.

Here I met Brother M——, and asked him how his wife was prospering. He said she was overrun with company, as whole wagon-loads often came from the country

to .spend the day. I said, "Mrs. M——
would not be imposed upon;" and, as the
good-natured clergyman laughed heartily, I
thought of what the rough frontiersman
who drove the horses when we were just
from the East and on our way to the border said: "You'll soon get used to this if
you stay in the West."

In the morning, after taking leave of our
good elder and his wife, I soon found myself seated in the railway-cars for the first
time for more than six years. But I was
not going East to visit my friends, as I had
often desired, but farther away from the
home of my childhood. It was long before day; my husband and my children had
fallen asleep; the car was but dimly lighted; a few passengers were half reclining
in their seats, and, as a thousand sorrow-
ful thoughts passed through my mind, I
could not refrain from weeping.

Shortly after sunrise the conductor passed through the car and cried out, "New-

ton." I wiped my eyes and looked out to see the little town where we left the cars and began our overland route over six years before this time, but I could not see it. The dozen little cabins were gone, and large brick buildings were standing in their places. Several church-spires were pointing toward the heavens. My six years' experience seemed to me like the dream of a night.

At the present time C—— is a fine railroad city surrounded by a beautiful and rich agricultural country. The little cabins and dug-outs have given way to pleasant residences, and many of those who lived so long on corn-bread and wild game are now able to cut the white loaf and live on the rich viands of the country. Where I have seen the buffalo, the deer and the wolf roaming at large, there are splendid roads, over which fine carriages daily roll; and where the deadly serpent stretched his form across the wild grapevine and moved noiselessly through the tall grass, stand beautiful orchards, fields of waving grain and lovely gardens. The little church which so long struggled in the midst of perils on every side now worships in a commodious sanctuary. The railroad not only brings a daily mail, but has brought down the prices of lumber, clothing, fuel and groceries. Excellent crops have this year been harvested, and the whole region abounds with plenty and prosperity. These people have well chosen for their motto *Ad astra per aspera.**

But, while this town and neighborhood have mounted to the bright stars of wealth through ten thousand difficulties, other towns far beyond are springing up, determined in like manner to go on through every difficulty to success and happiness. I know that hundreds of these places are without the blessed life-giving gospel of the Son of God. To-day the Macedonian cry,

* " Through hardships to the stars."

"Come over and help us," is ringing in the ears of the Church from more than a thousand dark and destitute fields in the great West. This soul-penetrating cry comes alike from the white man, the Indian and the Mexican, and cannot be disregarded with impunity.

While the Church, arrayed in garments of white, stands up and invites poor sinners to the Saviour, let her also reach out her hand and lead the weary and heavy-laden to his blessed feet. Who are willing to give up the pleasures of this life for Christ and his cause, and go among the poor and needy to bear afflictions as good soldiers of the cross? Who are willing to give as the Lord has prospered them for the support of this glorious work? "No man that warreth entangleth himself with the affairs of this life; that he may please Him who hath chosen him to be a soldier."

See the grain all ripe and falling,
Harvest ready : come and reap,

Jesus to his children calling,
 " Simon Peter, feed my sheep."

Hear the blessed Saviour saying,
 " In my vineyard work to-day;"
Hear the frontier settlers praying
 For the word without delay.

Hear the cry from Indian nation
 To the rich, the learned, the wise:
" Here poor Indians need salvation ;
 Bring us Christ, and we'll arise."

Hear the far-off Christian sister,
 In the land of waving green,
To her little children whisper,
 " You have ne'er a preacher seen."

See the drunkard as he tumbles
 In the ditch to moan and die ;
Who will whisper to that brother,
 " You through Christ may live on high " ?

Oh, my brother, oh, my sister,
 Can you sit and fold your hands,
While your days are passing swifter
 Than the river o'er the sands ?

THE END.

www.ingramcontent.com/pod-product-compliance
Lightning Source LLC
Chambersburg PA
CBHW030125030726
47498CB00007B/2558